Marbella Jack 3

By

Alan Evans

This book is dedicated to the memory

of

The Legendary Stevie 'O'

and

The Mighty Billy Outlaw

Friends who made life worth living

Shadow Men to the end

Ultimate warriors who will never be forgotten

Index

Chapter 1... Life goes on

Chapter 2... The Irish connection

Chapter 3... Passport to success

Chapter 4... The elusive torah

Chapter 5... The tobacco trail

Chapter 6... The masked assassin

Chapter 7... Friendly fire

Chapter 8... Disney matter

Chapter 9... Mine of confusion

Chapter 10... Traitors beware

Marbella Jack 3

Chapter 1

It had been six days now since the shooting, and Jack had lain almost motionless in his hospital bed. Sandra had only left the room for a moment to fetch a glass of water and when she returned she noticed that Jack had moved a little from the position that he was previously in, as she watched over him his eye lids flickered as he tried to cope with the brightness of the room, Sandra mopped his brow gently as she whispered softly to him. 'Jack, can you hear me, Jack.'

There was no answer to her question although Jacks eyes were now open.

'Can you hear me Jack?' She whispered as she stroked his hand.

'Where am I?' he groaned.

Sandra smiled 'Thank God.' She muttered, 'You're in hospital.'

'Why?' Jack breathed.

'Can't you remember?' she whispered.

'No' Jack grunted.

'You had an accident at home and I had you brought here.' She half lied so as not to worry him.

There was no reply from Jack, she saw that his eyes were closed and he had drifted off back to sleep. Sandra sat there stroking his hand and worrying whether he'd be okay. Jack woke several times during the night but only for a few seconds then he would drift back into the unconscious. The next morning Sandra wiped his forehead as he opened his eyes once more.
'Hiya babe' he whispered.
'Hiya honey,' she replied 'How ya feeling?'
'I'm okay.' He whispered.
Sandra knew that he was weak but at least now it looked like he was over the worst of the problems she was now hopeful that he would make a full recovery given time. 'You'll be okay hon.' she assured him.
'I know.' he half smiled.
Jack looked around the room and specifically at the clutter of hospital equipment and to the tubes that were attached to his body.
'What happened hon?'
'I'm not sure exactly, I only know that someone shot you through the window, and I found you on the floor bleeding; I called an ambulance and you've been here ever since.'
'What do ya mean ever since? Since when?'
'You've been here a few days.'
'I assume the odd lot have stuck their beaks in.' Jack whispered.
'They harassed me a lot at first, and then they went away and said they'd be back once you'd

woken up.

'What the fuck can I tell them? I know less than you and if I did know anything they're the last people I'd be talking to, the cheeky bastards.'

'Shhhhhush, don't get excited, let's get you better then I can get you home.'

'Sure hon sure.'

A little later Jack drifted off to sleep and Sandra went home to get changed and freshen up so that she would be ready to return later.

When Sandra returned to the hospital and walked into Jacks room, Charles was sat by Jacks bed they were talking quietly.

'Ahem,' Sandra coughed to let them know that she was there, they both said hello to her as she walked towards them; Sandra leaned forward and kissed Jack, Jack smiled. Sandra said, 'If you two are talking business, I'll go and get some coffees.

'No, nothing much left to say,' replied Charles.

'No, nothing.' added Jack.

'I'll get some coffee anyway.' She said. 'I'll be back in a minute, by the way while I remember some guy called Soapy rang; he wishes you well and he'll be in touch soon.' Sandra left the room closing the door behind her as she left. When she returned with her coffee Charles had gone. 'I've not frightened him off have I hon?

She laughed. 'Not much chance of that he's got some people to see.'

'Hmmm,' Sandra mused 'I see you've got the energy to talk to other people have you got any for me?'

'He's not other people.' Jack whispered.

Sandra looked at Jack; Jack smiled and fluttered his eyelids. Sandra put her coffee down and sat at the side of Jacks bed holding his hand.

'Who's trying to kill you Jack?' she asked quietly.

'Everyone by the look of it.'

'Have you got any ideas at all?'

'I think the list will be long and definite answers will still be none.'

'None.' she exclaimed.

'Well there have been no threats as such that I can think of, no reason that I can think of why someone would want to take a pot shot at me, but then again someone must be a bit upset to try again so soon after the killing of the mighty Outlaw, which goes to show the murder of Outlaw was an error on their part; so I've either upset someone big style or someone believes that I have, either way it's serious shit and I'll have to find a solution one way or another if I can.

'Before it's too late you mean.'

'Well there's always that for an incentive.'

The door opened abruptly Jacks eyes sharpened and Sandra looked around at the

man walking into the room. It was Pete carrying a bunch of flowers. 'Flowers Pete, are you going soft?'
'Well ya know hospitals an all that.'
'Hmmmm.' Smirked Jack.
'How ya doin Jack? Pete asked.
'How am I fuckin doing, how does it look like I'm doing? Tubes and machines attached to me all over the fuckin show.'
'I was only being polite.'
'Well try thinking before you ask any daft questions you fuckin gommack.'
'No need to be insulting Jack.' Said the now embarrassed Pete. 'I'm sorry mate, I'm just pissed off with all this bollox.'
'Any ideas Jack?'
'We've just been through all that, plenty of suspects but nothing definite.'
'Can't think of anyone meself other than the usual and the obvious.' Pete mused.
'Same as us then, nothing.'
'Looks like it.' They all talked a while longer until the nurse came in and asked them to let Jack have some rest for a while; Pete said that he'd be back soon and left; Sandra kissed Jack goodbye then left the room following Pete along the corridor. The nurse changed the dressings on Jacks wounds; then she gave him a pain relieving injection; Jack was asleep in seconds.
The next day Jack awoke bright and early and

although he couldn't manage all of his breakfast he did manage some and that was a good start to the day. A few hours later a doctor came in and asked Jack how he was feeling Jack said that he was okay; the doctor then took the chart from the bottom of the bed and turning his back to Jack he began to read it, then in a flash like a scene from a horror movie the doctor spun around and plunged a knife into Jack's already wounded body, Jack screamed out and tried to struggle with his attacker, a nurse who was passing the room rushed in and confronted the attacker, she was stabbed in the stomach for her troubles; at that moment Pete turned up to visit Jack and walked right into the bloodbath, Jack was hanging out of the bed covered in blood the nurse was on the floor bleeding Jack was trying to hang on to his attacker, Pete also tried to tackle the assailant but was thrown to the floor; Pete got back up just in time to be punched full in the face which sent him tumbling backwards once more and the murderous `doctor' used the opportunity to make good his escape, Jacks previously tidy room looked like something from a war zone, Pete crawled into the hospital corridor to raise the alarm, and people came running to their assistance. Jack and the nurse were taken to separate operating theatres.
It was some days later when Jack finally came around and as his eyes finally found focus on his surroundings the first thing he saw was

Sandra she just stared at him with tears in her eyes, Jack tried to talk to her but he couldn't find the strength. 'Why?' Sandra cried.
Jack could do nothing but stare back at his crying wife his mind to muddled through pain killing drugs to string any thoughts together it wasn't long before he drifted back off into the land of nod. Sandra stayed for a while before going home to see that their children were alright. The police had now left a twenty-four hour guard on Jacks room, the fact that two attempts on his life had now been made and there was the likelihood of another if past history was anything to go by; that and the untimely death of the Outlaw all these events had to be taken into account, this is what had prompted the police into action. The police were also waiting to talk to Jack once he had woken properly.

It was another three weeks later before the doctor agreed that the police could interview Jack, by then Jack was sat up in his bed, not exactly comfortable but much better than he had been since his second attack. The police entered Jacks room 'Well we seem to be running into each other quite a lot just lately Dunkerley.'

'Not by any choice of mine.'

'Right, lets not beat about the bush, what can you tell me about the first attack when you were shot at home?'

'Nothing.'
'Nothing.' The cop re-iterated.
'I can't remember a single thing.'
'Right, well how about a motive, someone with a grudge?'
'No-one springs to mind.' Jack said truthfully.
'Well we don't seem to be getting very far on that one, so how about the second attack here in this hospital when you and two other people were attacked and injured?'
'All I know is that a doctor came into the room and started to read my chart then like a flash he turned and attacked me.'
'What did he look like?'
'A doctor.'
'Can you describe him?'
'He had a white coat on.'
'You're a mine of information Dunkerley.'
'Thanks.'
'What else do you know?'
'Absolutely nothing.'
'Fucking marvelous, we're trying to protect you and you're protecting whoever it is who is attacking you, the nurse the other feller and possibly whoever it was who murdered Billy Outlaw.'
'Listen lets get a couple of things right, I've not asked for your help, I don't know who it is whose attacking me otherwise they wouldn't be doing it, certainly not more than once anyway.'
'Maybe they're smarter than you.'

'Maybe they are.'
'So what's your next move?'
'To go to sleep.'
'Forever the smartarse eh Dunkerley.'
'One tries.'
The interviewing policeman turns to his colleague and says, 'Lets go, we're wasting our time here.' Both the men got up and headed for the door, one of them said, 'I'll be back.'
'Not another Arnold.' Jack mumbled.
'What was that?'
'Nothing, just nothing.'
'Well if you remember anything.'
'Yeah, right.' Jack smiled.
A few days later Jack went home from the hospital, he was happy to get back to the comforts of his own home and more than happy to off load the police guard that he'd had forced upon him. Pete called round to Jacks house for a chat. 'What the fuck is all this about Jack is there something that I should I know?'
'Not that I know of Pete.' Jack replied answering the last question first.
'Its certainly got me confused Jack, I've run out of fuckin ideas mate, I can't think of anything that's happened over the last few years that would cause this much shit.'
'Well that's two of us feller, that's definitely two of us.' Sandra brought in some tea as the two men chatted away incessantly; Sandra retreated to the kitchen to sort out Jacks newly enforced

diet.

Two days later Jack returned to the hospital to have the stitches removed from his stomach wound, while he was there they also changed the dressing on the wounds from the previous attack; Jack asked about the nurse that had been injured whilst trying to save him from the attack by the bogus doctor he was told that she was on the way to full recovery. Sandra was driving Jack back home from the hospital when Jack had a brainwave. 'Take me to Pete's hon.'

'Pete's, ...what for?'

'Just a little chat.' he grinned.

Here we go again thought Sandra as she changed lanes on the carriageway preparing herself for the next junction and a different direction from the one that she thought she'd be going in. Sandra got out of the car at Pete's house, she walked to the door and rang the bell; Jack waited in the car not wanting to make the effort in case Pete wasn't in. Pete answered the door and was surprised to see Sandra standing there, before he could speak Sandra said, 'Jacks in the car.'

'Is he' Pete exclaimed.

Pete looked over towards the car to see Jack struggling to get out of the open door, by the time Pete and Sandra had walked down the Path to the car Jack was fully out of the car and standing up in what looked to both of them as an uncomfortable position, with help from the

others Jack hobbled up the Path and into the house. Jack turned to Sandra and said, 'Pick me up in an hour hon.'
Sandra not being one who needed telling twice and not wanting to be a witness to any untoward conversations said her goodbyes and left
'Well Pete,' Jack declared. 'Where do we go from here?'
'Fuck knows Jack its all a bleedin mystery to me.'
'How's business for a start?'
'Fuckin dreadful, with all this hassle I've hardly been doin a thing.'
'We need to take care of business Pete we've got people relying on us to keep their families fed.'
'Jack .... The main priority is to fuckin well stay alive.'
'Well it is always a positive sign when ya wake up in a morning.' 'Well if ya don't mate everything else is downhill.'
'Yep, it's always a bad start to the day waking up dead.' Jack laughed.
'Yeah mate not very good for business at all.'
'Okay, now we've established that we're still alive, we need to work out what our next move is.'
'I'm just waiting on you Jack.'
'I thought you might be, for a start we need to make sure that our customers are properly serviced so that we've got some money coming

in; once we're up and running again we can concentrate on who it is who is trying to kill me and who it was who killed Billy Outlaw.'
'Where are you going to start?'
'I've not got a fuckin clue yet, but if we spread enough money around someone will eventually be tempted to tell.'
'And when they do?'
The two men looked at each other without saying a word for a moment, then Pete said 'Must be fuckin psychic us Jack.'
'I wish, ... what else do you know?'
'Phil's been nicked.'
'Which Phil?'
'Phil from the Garage.'
'Fuckinell, how did that happen?'
'Well Jack I heard that some undercover cop approached him and started selling him cigs and booze, that went on for a few months and the undercover cop kept trying to get him into other things Phil wouldn't have it at first but they drew him in then stitched him up like a kipper now he's nicked and he's on remand at Doncatraz.'
'What a shower of shit those fuckers are but that's what they do, it's a nationally corrupt squad classic; they approach the target they get him interested in some half illegal enterprise where he can make a few quid like the cigs and booze racket, then they draw him into doing something a bit or a lot more risky than he

would have done on his own then just before the job goes down the first cop introduces another undercover pretend lorry driver then the first one drops out leaving the second cop to do the pick ups and the drop offs; the crime squad organise the transport, the drugs, they make all the arrangements from start to finish but involving the target victim just enough to get a conviction then they walk away laughing or so they think.'

'The bunch of cunts.'

'Yeah, they're not capable of catching a cold on their own so they set people up to make themselves look good.'

'So that's why they're called the national crime squad?'

'Why?'

'Coz they create crimes.'

'Yep, they sure do and most of the time they get away with it, the dirty bastards.'

'Sad old world Jack innit?'

'Sadder than most people think mate.'

'Yeah I suppose you're right Jack.'

'I am, but that's not helping us; where are we up to business wise?'

'Well with our recent disasters we're pretty much in the shit, I've been buying the puff over here just to keep our customers happy but the profit is dismal.'

'Fuckin marvellous.'

'Its not been our best year we've had one of our

best men murdered and the boss as been shot to fuck, and on top of that I'm getting a fuckin ulcer.'
'A minor triviality for a man of your talents Pete.'
'I'm also getting the serious heebee jeebees about the whole fuckin show.'
'Hey, don't go bottling out on me now Pete.'
'I'm not, I just need to give my nerves a rest it's been mega stressful just lately.'
'Tell me about it.'
Pete heard a car pulling up outside his house; he got up and walked towards the window.
'It's Sandra.' Pete declared.
'Fuckinell, that was a quick hour.'
'Wannit.'
'Right Pete I'll have a think about what we can do next.'
'Okay mate.'
Jack hobbled towards the door and as the doorbell rang Pete who was already there opened it to the startled Sandra. 'Is he ready,' Sandra asked. 'I'm coming, I'm coming.' Jack answered before Pete could get his words out. 'I'll be in touch.' Jack muttered as he squeezed out of the door. 'Soon as you can Jack we need to get rolling.'
'I know mate believe me I know.'
Jack and Sandra said their goodbyes as they walked towards their car. They were half way home when Sandra said, 'Penny for your

thoughts?'
'Sorry, what?'
'You're thoughts Jack a penny for them, you were daydreaming or at least in some form of deep meditation.'
'Yeah right, just thinking hon.'
'We'll soon be home.'
'Hmmmm I can feel a brew coming on.'
'Didn't you have one at Petes?'
'That's not quite the same as one of yours hon.' Jack grinned. 'Not quite eh.' Sandra mumbled.
Twelve days later Jack met up with Pete and explained that he'd been in touch with the `A' team and they were willing to supply them again at the going rate and using the same system as they'd used before. Pete complained that there wasn't enough money in doing business that way to make it worthwhile especially in the long term. 'Who said anything about long term.'
'What else?'
'We'll have to look at some different sources of income.'
'Yeah, like what?'
'Like whatever comes up cigs, booze, armed robbery.'
'Armed fuckin robbery.' Pete nearly choked on the words.
'Only jesting Pete that might be a bit to much,…..even for us.'
'A fuckin lot to much if you ask me.'

'I always ask you Pete.'
'Hmmm, how about if we organise another importation?'
'Great if we could get one that works.' Pete grinned.
'Well we can give it some thought, plus I can speak to some other people to see if they've got any ideas.'
'Talking of ideas, any new thoughts on who the shooter is or where it's coming from?' Pete asked.
'Still not a clue mate but I've got my feelers out and I'm confident that an answer will be coming soon.'
'I hope so coz at the moment I can't trust anyone.'
'Keep it like that and you won't go far wrong.' Jack stressed.
'I'd rather have some fuckin peace my nerves are shot.'

The two men parted company and Jack started to look into other ways of importing his duty free goods. He trundled through the vast amount of names and numbers that he had tucked away for emergencies, a name jumped from the page `Roger' he thought aloud, I wonder what he's up to these days; later that day Jack phoned Roger and arranged to meet him two days later for a little chat.
'Long time no see Jack.'

'Aye my friend it is, I see you've sneaked a few pounds on.'
'Good living.' He laughed while Patting his protruding belly.
The two men soon got settled in each others company, Roger told Jack about the scams he'd been doing and Jack explained not in to much detail about some of the things he'd been doing and ending on the sad note of Outlaws death and the two other recent attempts on his own life. 'What's it all about?' asked Roger.
'Fuck knows, maybe we'll never know.'
'Aren't you worried about them coming back for another go?'
'All the fuckin time, but I can't sit about waiting for something to happen that might never occur, I can't sit in a bullet proof room twenty four hours a day.'
'Suppose not mate but you'd better be careful.'
'Oh I am Roger, believe me I am.'
Roger explained that he'd been involved in the cig business but now that some of his buyers had been arrested and the contact that used to organise the papers being signed had been sacked, he was now looking at other ways to develop his business. 'How were you smuggling the cigs in?' enquired Jack.
'We weren't.'
'What do you mean?'
'We were pretending to export them, then getting the paperwork sorted out to say that the

load had arrived at its destination, and we were laughing all the way to the bank.'

'It fuckingwell sounds like it too.'

'Oh happy days Jack, happy fuckin days.'

'I wouldn't mind a bit of that myself.' said Jack thoughtfully.

'It's no problem for me to get the cigs you just need someone in the right position in one of the right countries to sign the papers and we'll all be laughing all the way to the bank.'

'Now that would be nice, I'll see what I can do and I'll get back to you.' Jack got into his car and headed for home, a million thoughts swirling around in his head, more than enough to put the average man in the nut house. 'Stress, stress and more stress.' Jack mumbled to himself.

The following day Jack went to meet Pete to explain that he was going away to Spain to meet with Seamus his old friend to see if he could put a deal together. 'I'll be back in a few days.'

'Yeah, no problem.'

'Will you manage without me?'

'Oh, I'll scrape by at a push.' Pete laughed.

'Just like normal then eh?'

'Hey don't be taking the piss or I'll be fuckin shootin ya next.'

'Don't be getting personal, it's only a little jest.'

'Hmmmmm.'

Pete didn't add anything to his little mumble, so the two men said their goodbyes and parted

company.
Two days later Jack walked off the aeroplane into the warm night air of Malaga, there to meet him was Seamus and another Irishman another old friend of Jacks called Toby, they greeted each other like long lost brothers then after a few minutes they piled into Seamus' car and headed out of the airport towards the southern coast. Jack was to be staying in the spare room at Seamus' villa and after a short drive along the Paseo Maritimo to view the chicas the men slipped into the Hollywood nights restaurant on fuengirola marina to be entertained by the singer Zak as they enjoyed their meals. 'Where to next?' declared Seamus.
'Bed for me, I'm knackered. Yawned Jack.
'The nights young.' Shouted Toby.
'For you maybe, but I'm not used to it these days.
'Anyone for the ninety two?' asked Toby.
'I couldn't raise a laugh.' Jack laughed.
'Nor me.' Said Seamus.
'What the fucks up with you two?' moaned Toby.
'We got old.' Smiled Jack, and Seamus nodded in agreement, then said 'But we've got some good memories haven't we Jack.' The two men laughed.
Before Jack could make comment Toby Butted in with 'Fuck the memories I want some fuckin action.'

'No problem,' said Seamus, 'You take the car and we'll grab a taxi and we'll see you up at my place later.'
'That's okay but I don't want to walk into a fuckin brothel on my own.'
Seamus said that there was plenty of bars between here and there and that he was bound to recruit at least a couple of guys that he knew to go with him.'
'Yeah okay,' he said, 'I'll catch up with you two later.' Toby picked up the car keys off the table and wandered off out of the restaurant. The two remaining men having paid the bill took a walk out of the restaurant onto the marina then around past Lineker's bar where all the young kids were hanging about having fun, then up onto the Paseo before calling in the London pub for another drink, alcohol for Seamus but Jack was still on the britvic orange, they perused the body's of the young dancing girls before pushing their way through the crowd to the door and back onto the Paseo where there was always a queue of taxis waiting to alleviate some unsuspecting tourist of a bundle of his or her holiday money. The two men clambered into a taxi and headed for Seamus' villa, it was made clear to the taxi driver not to take any tourist routes. The now tired Jack was looking forward to climbing into bed and disappearing into the land of nod until at least the next afternoon; the warm night air

and the traumas of the long day had taken their toll on Jacks body he was soon in a deep sleep. Jack was still tired when he got out of bed the next morning the heat of the Spanish night coupled with the unfamiliar bed caused him to have a restless night. Jack searched around in the kitchen for tea bags whilst the kettle boiled. The sound of the kettle whistling caused Seamus to force open his eyes to the morning light, he crawled out of his bed and headed for the bathroom, Jack on hearing movement and the closing of the bathroom door shouted out;
'Where do you keep the tea bags?'
'They're in the bread bin.'
'That fuckin figures.' Jack muttered to himself. Jack made two cups of tea and took them out onto the Patio where he sat and waited for Seamus to appear, which he did some moments later.
'That fuckin suns bright.' Seamus declared as he popped his head around the Patio door.
'Best put some shades on then.'
'Yeah, good idea.'
Two minutes later Seamus resurfaced with his previously screwed up eyes now covered with snide Rayban shades.
'Did ya buy a job lot?'
'Job lot, what do ya mean?'
'I mean the snide shades.'
'What do you mean snide …I paid good money for these.'

'Then you've been robbed mate.'
'It'll not be the first time.' He moaned.
They both grinned at each other.
'Or the last.' they said in unison before Bursting into laughter.
'What are you two laughing about?' said the now awakened Toby standing with a towel over his head.
'You got no snide Raybans then Tobe?' Jack asked, as he and Seamus tried to contain their laughter without much success.
`Funny old world' thought Jack.
'What's on the menu today then chaps?' asked Seamus.
'Some breakfast followed by some deep and meaningful conversation, which hopefully will become actions and turn into cash somewhere down the road.' Mused Jack.
'I'll have some of that.' said the man in the Raybans thoughtfully. The three men arrived at the Starlight cafe on the Paseo Maritimo and ordered their English breakfasts. 'Fancy a game of pool?' asked Seamus.
'It's a bit early in the day for me; my eyes are only just opening properly.' Jack grinned.
'Should get yourself some Raybans mate.' Laughed Seamus.
'You wouldn't know a Rayban from a fuckin driving ban.' Jack chuckled.
'Yeah, I would, them driving bans last longer.' Seamus joked. The three men laughed and got

up to take turns to play pool while they waited for their breakfasts to arrive, once it had arrived it didn't take long for the hungry men to devour the long awaited anti anorexia meal. During the meal Seamus' mobile phone had rang, he'd answered it quickly and told the caller that he was eating his breakfast and that he'd ring them back later, and now that they'd finished eating he was back on the telephone chatting away and making arrangements to meet someone later that day. Seamus paid the bill and the three men walked out of the cafe onto the Paseo, Jack and Toby followed Seamus towards the parked car.
'Pile in chaps we're off to Marbella.'

'Marbella eh! Now this could be interesting.' Jack muttered.

'It will be, we've got a meeting with some chaps that I'm sure you'll like to meet.' Said the now jolly Seamus.

'Even more interesting.' Replied the deeply in thought Jack.

Toby as usual took everything in his stride and said nothing he just trundled along going with the flow, as was his normal attitude to life.

Half an hour later they pulled onto the massive car park of the Las Canadas shopping centre, they parked the car and walked across the car park to the MacDonald's entrance, where they entered the overfull cafe come restaurant Seamus waved at two men that he obviously knew to follow him and they all left by

another door which led into the main shopping centre, the five men stood around being introduced and shaking hands. 'Let's find somewhere to sit down.' Said Seamus. The five men wandered through the busy shopping centre 'Up there.' Seamus pointed. The other men looked up to the second floor area, which encircled part of the shopping centre. 'There's a bar up there.'
'Sounds okay to me.' Said the thirsty Jack
'And us.' One of the others muttered.
The bar was very quiet, especially considering how busy the rest of the place was, the drinks arrived and once the waiter was out of earshot one of the two men that Seamus had brought to the meeting started to talk. He explained to Jack that there were two possible deals on the table one being that he could arrange shipments of tax free cigarettes out of Gibraltar back to England or that he could set up fake companies importing cigarettes to Gibraltar direct from cigarette companies in England the first one would have to be a major smuggling operation out of Gibraltar then across Spain and France eventually having to avoid capture on the English borders the other way is where the cigarettes never leave England in the first place but all the paperwork is put in place and stamped up so that it looks like a legal transaction. 'Sounds okay in theory, but the downside hasn't been looked at.' Said Jack.

'What fuckin downside?' barked Seamus.
'There's always a fuckin downside.' Jack sighed.
'Is there?'
'Absolutely always.' Said the thoughtful Jack. Jack asked the two men the ins and outs of all these transactions he spent over an hour questioning their ideas and methods and adding some suggestions himself, when he was eventually satisfied that he had all the information that he needed he stood up and shook hands with the two men and said that he'd be back in touch with them as soon as he had looked into all the matters that they'd discussed, with that the two men said their goodbyes and walked off into the shopping centre. Jack sat back down and called to the waiter to bring more drinks. 'What do ya reckon Jack?' asked Seamus. 'I reckon we'll give it some thought.'
'Give it some thought, ... is that it?'
'For now, so where we off to now?'
'Some food wouldn't go amiss.' Said the previously silent Toby. 'Do you only think of your belly?' said Seamus.
'When it's empty I do.' Said Toby while Patting his stomach.
'Empty, after that breakfast you ate this morning.' Laughed Jack.
'Twas a long time ago and I'm starving.' Said the hungry man.
'By the time we get out of here and back to

fuengirola we'll all be hungry, we can have one of them big steaks at that German restaurant next door to Hollywood nights. Seamus teased.
'Sounds right to me.' said Jack.
'I'm drooling.' Said the starving Toby while licking his lips. The remaining three men finished their drinks quickly and on leaving the cafe headed for the car. Back in fuengirola half an hour later they struggled to find somewhere to park on the marina so that they could eat at the German restaurant; with Toby continually moaning how hungry he was they managed to park the vehicle and then trying to keep up with Toby's brisk pace they headed past Linekers bar towards the front of the marina where they caught up with Toby outside The German steakhouse. 'Fuckin closed.' Toby shouted, causing several passers by to turn and look.
'It's closed,' Seamus muttered, 'I'm hungry meself now.'
'About turn then,' said Jack, 'I know just the place.'
'Not more greasy fuckin breakfast?' Seamus declared.
'No, a nice roast dinner at Jumbo's on the paseo.'
'Yeah, I know the place.' Seamus nodded.
'Will it be open at this time?' pleaded the ravenous Toby.
'We'll soon see.' Said Jack; as they all piled back into the car.

A few minutes later the three men wandered into Jumbo's restaurant and sat at a table. 'What are you having chaps?' asked Jack.
'Food, food and more food.' Said the now grinning Toby.
They all ordered meals and sat around waiting, Toby rather more impatient than the other two, Jack and Seamus were whispering to each other about the possible deals that had been discussed earlier in Marbella. Toby was more interested in eating than listening. The starters arrived and the plates had hardly touched the table before Toby had a mouthful of food, Jack thought if Toby had been any quicker he'd have taken chunks out of the waitress's hand, he laughed to himself so as not to cause any offence. Two days later Seamus took Jack to Malaga airport where Jack caught a flight back to England.
`Keep in touch' were Seamus' last words before Jack went through the airports security gate, Jack said that he would ring him as soon as there was any development. Jack telephoned Pete from the airport while he was waiting for Sandra to collect him; He arranged to meet up with him later at the Mucky Duck. Firstly though Jack wanted to go home and spend some time alone with Sandra. They barely had an hour together before Sandra had to dash off to collect the children from school. Jack had other plans; he went to see his brother Charles for a brief chat before some time later making his

way down to the Mucky Duck to meet up with Pete. Jack and Pete sat at a table in the corner of the pub away from the crowded bar so that they could talk in peace; Jack explained the two deals to Pete and as always Pete was taking in every last detail; He knew that if any of these deals were to come into fruition then he would be somewhere in the firing line and he didn't want to be making any mistakes. 'Where do we go from here?' asked Pete.

'I'm not sure mate, I'll have to speak to a few of my contacts and if anything develops we'll get on an earner, if not then it's back to square one.'

'Nothing new then.' Pete grinned.

Jack laughed, 'No nothing new then.' Jack's mobile phone rang, it was Sandra 'Where are you?'

'I'm at my girlfriends.'

'Many a true word said in jest.'

'Now calm down, I'm in the pub with Pete we're just about to have a meal.'

'Oh, are you now, and I've just made your tea.'

'I'll be home shortly then.'

'What about your meal?'

'It's only a bag of crisps Pete can have mine.'

'You're a bar steward, winding me up all the time.'

'Got to keep you on your toes hon.'

'Hmmmm we'll see about that, how long will you be?'

'I'm leaving now, so give me fifteen minutes.'

'Okay, I'll have a brew ready, so don't be any longer.'
'Okeydoke.' Jack said as he turned off his phone and after turning to say goodbye to Pete he left.
The next day Jack went to see his old friend Angel who was definitely into making a few quid if the risk and the jail time were both limited. 'Well who isn't' thought Jack to himself as he trundled up to Angels door. The big Irishman opened the door and with a big grin he said, 'Ah, its Jack the lad'
'Get it right ya fat bastard it's Jack the young lad.'
'Oh it's Jack the young lad now is it?'
'And getter younger by the minute mate.'
'I'll have some of whatever you're taking.'
'You wish.' Said Jack as he followed Angel into his house.
'What can I do you for?' asked Angel plonking himself into the Captains chair at his office desk and tilting the chair so as to find himself a comfortable position. Jack sat down and talked to him about the cigarette business and the possibilities and dangers of smuggling from Gibraltar back to England he also discussed with Angel the scam that Angel had told him about quite some time ago and they'd agreed that it was possible if the right people were in place to organise the paperwork. 'A nice touch if you can pull it off.' Said Angel

'This is how it is going to work.' Jack said as he explained his plans to the ever more interested Angel. Jack went over all the main points of both of the scams even the tiniest details were discussed such as what would be needed, who would be doing what, where and how; plus how long it would take and what the outlay would be compared to the returns; Every point was mulled over time and again until there was nothing left to say; the two men agreed to part company while they each checked that their own ends could be met; they arranged to meet again a few days later, Jack said that he'd ring and let him know when that would be. The two men parted company at Angel's front door. Jack went to his car, got in and drove home.

Chapter Two

Some days later Pete rang Jack to let him know that he had a little problem and he would need to meet with him to see if Jack could help him to resolve it; the two men met up a few hours later to discuss the issue, Pete explained that he'd let a Turkish guy that he knew have fifty kees of puff on credit the problem arose when the Turkish guy had been ripped off for the gear and couldn't trace his so called friend who had taken responsibility for the puff.
'What are we going to do about it Jack?'
'I'm not sure.'
'I feel a bit guilty about it.'
'It's not your fault Pete.'
'I still don't feel good about it though.'
'Don't worry about it Pete, we'll sort it.'
'How?'
'I'm not sure, can you arrange a meet for me with your Turk?'
'I'll speak to him, but he'll be worried about meeting anyone after losing the puff.' 'Just see what you can do, tell him it's just a chat to try to resolve the problem.' 'Okay Jack, I'll work on it.'
'Right, I'll catch up with ya later mate, I've got things to do.'

The two men parted company and Jack went to see Angel to see if he had any news on the cig business. 'I'm still working on it Jack.' Said the rather stressed Angel as he was trying to balance two phones under his chin at the same time and fiddle with the keyboard on his computer. He put the phones down on his desk and turned to Jack saying, 'I'm having a bad day.'
'I'm having lots of bad days mate.'
'You got problems too?'
'Haven't we all?'
'Suppose I'm not on my own then?'
'Me, you and half the world mate.'
'It still doesn't make me feel any better.'
'No, I didn't suppose it would, but I thought I'd let you know anyway.' Jack grinned.
'Ya cantankerous bastard.'
'Now if that ain't the kettle calling the pot black.'
'Pot, don't mention pot in here, the Mrs will be on my case.' The two men laughed in unison.
'Funny old world innit?'
'Yeah, innit?'
Jack then having got no further with his inroads into the cig smuggling enterprise left Angels house and headed for home. Later that day Pete rang Jacks house 'Hello Jack.'
'Hello, what's happening?'
'Are ya busy tomorrow?'
'Not that I know of, why?'

'I'll pick you up at ten in the morning.'
'Where are we going?'
'Leicester.'
'Leicester.' Jack reiterated.
'Yep, Leicester, we've got a meeting.'
'Right, right, I'm with ya, I'll see ya in the morning then.'
'Okay, ten o'clock.'
'Ten o'clock then, bye.'
'Bye.'
Jack put the telephone receiver down then wandered thoughtfully into his kitchen to make himself a coffee.
The next morning Jack paced up and down his kitchen drinking coffee while waiting for the elusive Pete to arrive it was nearly ten thirty when Pete finally knocked on Jacks door.
 'Where the fuck have you been?' demanded Jack has he opened the door to the red faced Pete. 'I er overslept.'
'Overslept,' Jack muttered, 'I've been ringing your house for ages and your fuckin mobile.'
'I must have left the house before you rang and the battery's flat on the mobile.'
'A real professional outfit this,' Jack Shouted, 'oversleeping, flat batteries you're making us look like a right pair of prats.'
'Sorry Jack.'
'Come on get in the car.' Jack growled.
'Right, right.'
'No, not that door, get in the other side, I'll

drive.'

'Is there a reason for that.'

'Yeah, so that we've got half a fuckin chance of getting there.'

'Thanks.' Said the embarrassed Pete.

The two men carried on their journey in silence until they reached the outskirts of Leicester when Jack had to ask Pete for directions to the venue of the meeting. They eventually found the house that they were looking for and Pete went to the door and knocked while Jack sat in the car, the door of the house opened and Pete went in; a few minutes later Pete reappeared at the door and waved to Jack to come into the house. Jack walked into the dimly lit hallway and followed Pete down a narrow corridor into a back room that was barely furnished, there was a thread worn rug slung unevenly in the middle of the floor; `This is hardly the surroundings of the successful' thought Jack as he walked into the room and was beckoned by a small gaunt looking man to sit down; Jack looked at the state of the furniture and was worried by two things one being that he'd never get his trousers clean ever again and the other more worrying was whether this dilapidated furniture would take his weight; he had visions of passing straight through this old settee in one fell swoop like a chain saw through balsa wood leaving him lying in a heap on the floor. Jack not wanting to seem unfriendly lowered himself slowly and gently onto the now loudly creaking seat. 'Would you like some tea?' asked the skeletal man. 'No, no not for me thanks.' said Jack hurriedly while pondering the conditions of where it was likely to come from. 'I'll have some.' Said the unobservant Pete, Plonking himself into a chair.

The Turkish man shouted utterings in a foreign language into a corridor that obviously led to another room, a few minutes later a little old lady appeared in the room carrying a tray with strange looking tea and even stranger looking biscuits on it. 'Are you sure you won't have any?' asked the Turkish man. 'Yeah, I'm fine.' Jack said as he struggled to keep his face straight at the weird look that was now on Pete's face as the Turkish man gave him his cup of tea and insisted on Pete having some of the odd looking biscuits. Jack thought that Pete was starting to look ill, he bit his lip harder to try to hide any feelings of laughter that were brewing, the last thing that he needed now was to fall about laughing, the furniture probably couldn't take it anyway he thought. Jack coughed loudly and purposely to take control of the situation.

'Ahem, right, let's get down to business.' He said.

The Turkish man explained that his contact, another Turk had taken the fifty kees away to sell and had arranged to return the following

day but he hadn't been seen since and that had been a week ago; Jack asked the Turk how he was going to pay the bill and the only solution the Turk could come up with was to offer Jack heroin in exchange for the money that he owed.
'We don't touch heroin, not for money, not for debt, not for anything, for us it's a no, no.'
'We only mess with a bit of puff.' Pete added. The Turk sat there listening saying nothing, just nodding his head in agreement with the two men's comments. 'The only other solution then, he said, was to wait until I've sold the stuff myself then I will be able to pay.'
'It sounds the sensible idea to me.' Jack answered.
'It may take a week or two.'
'As long as it's not much longer, then we can survive.'
The Turk went on to talk about other subjects that he wished to discuss with Jack of the many things that he talked about, the one he seemed really interested in was passports; Jack said that he'd have a word with a few of his contacts once he'd been paid for the puff and only then would he get back to him. The Turk took note of Jacks frankness. It was only four days later when the Turk rang Pete and told him that he had the necessary paperwork and that he would send a man down to Pete's area later that day he said that he'd phone back later with the exact details. Pete phoned Jack and

arranged to meet at the Mucky Duck.
'What's occurring Pete? asked Jack.
'Just thought I'd let you know that the Turk is sending that money down today.'
'That's good news, I didn't expect him to deliver so quick.'
'Maybe his missing friend reappeared.'
'Maybe, ...right Pete, let me know when he's been and gone and the necessary has been checked.'
'Yeah, right Jack I'll get straight on to ya.'
'Right, I'm off to see a man about some cigs, I'll catch ya later.'
'Okay, later then.
The two men parted company and left the pub through different exits as they headed for their cars. An hour later Jack pulled onto the cash and carry car park, he left his car and headed for the offices. 'Can I help you sir?' asked the young Asian receptionist. 'Is the boss in?'
'Which one?'
'Mohammed will do fine.'
'I'll see if he's in, she declared, who shall I say is calling?' 'Jack Dunkerley.' Jack said casually.
The woman pressed buttons and spoke a foreign language into the microphone that was floating in front of her mouth on a wire that in turn was attached to her head; she turned to Jack and said, 'He'll be along shortly.'

No sooner had she spoken than one of the doors behind her opened and a dumpy little Asian man poked out his head and waved for Jack to enter his office. 'Well Jack, long time no see, what brings this pleasure?'
'I'm thinking about going into the cig business and I thought I'd ask your advice before I committed myself'
'I'm listening.'
Jack explained about the two methods of acquiring the cigs one way was by them being smuggled into the country and the other way of not being sent out in the first place. 'If and when I get my hands on them can you shift them on?' Jack enquired.
'That depends, said the half interested Mohammed, I can't shift them through my business because the packaging won't be correct for this country; I could probably shift them elsewhere to some people that I know, but then again that would depend on the price.'
'I'll get off for now, and I'll get back to you when I know more details myself, I just thought I'd see if you were interested before I commit myself.'
'I'm always interested in earning a penny or two.' Laughed the dumpy Mohammed.
Jack smiled, thinking this man wouldn't even draw breath for a penny or two.
The two men said their goodbyes and Jack

walked out of Mohammed's office into the reception area where he said goodbye to the young Asian girl as he passed by. Jack then drove to see Angel to see if he knew any more about the cig situation and on finding out that Angel was no further on with the cig job, Jack left and headed for home. 'It's been a long day, Sandra.' Jack said as he entered his house. Sandra walked into the hallway to meet him, putting her finger to her mouth to let him know not to speak she said, 'There's someone here to see you hon.'
'And who might that be.'
'The police.' She whispered.
Jack walked into his lounge. 'What do you want?' he snapped at the startled detective.
'I've just called to see if you've remembered anymore about the recent attacks on you and the nurse and of course the earlier attack on you, where Billy Outlaw was killed?'
'I've told you everything that I know.'
'That's not been a lot.'
'That's because I don't know a lot.'
'I think you know more than you're telling.'
'Well if I remember anything, I'll give you a call.'
'I'm sure,' Said the detective as he got up to leave, 'that nurse could have got killed trying to help you.'
'I know that.'
'But you're not willing to help?'

'I keep telling you, I don't know anything.'
'Yeah, right.' The detective mumbled something inaudible as he headed for Jacks front door and let himself out.
Sandra brought a cup of tea in for Jack.
'I see your friends gone.' She teased.
'He's not my fuckin friend.' Jack growled.
'Calm down Jack, I was only joking.'
'Nothing funny about having one of the fuckin Gestapo associated with ya, I'll tell ya that for nothing.'
'Okay, okay, message received loud and clear.' Sandra said as she wandered upstairs out of his way. Jack picked up Sandra's mobile and rang Pete. 'Hello Pete.'
'Yeah, who's that?'
'It's me.'
'Right,' Pete said realising who it was, 'What's up?'
'Nothing, I just wanted to know whether we ever sorted that nurse out? the one that got hurt when she helped me at the hospital.'
'You didn't tell me to.'
'Well I meant to, can you sort it?'
'Yeah Jack, how much should I give her?'
'I'll leave that to you, but she's been off work since the attack.'
'Okay, I'll sort it and I'll get back to ya.'
'Good man, I'll see ya soon, bye.'
'Bye Jack.' Pete said as he put his phone down.
It keeps him busy Jack thought, as he paced up

and down his lounge pondering about the days events, and wondering where all these twists and turns would eventually lead, at the very least it's not a boring life he convinced himself. The following day Jack went to a call box and telephoned Seamus; 'Anything happening on the western front yet Jack?'
'No, I'm still working on it, what I'm ringing about is something different, do you remember them little books you got a while ago from back home, you got a few for you and some of the lads?'
'No, you've lost me there mate.'
'The little books, the one with ya picture in it.'
'Gotcha Jack, you went a bit round the houses, didn't ya?
'Never know who's listening, do ya?'
'Still paranoid Jack?'
'Can't be to careful mate.'
'Suppose not, how many books do ya need?'
'I don't know.'
'Strange.'
'Not really, they're not for me there for ……..should we say a friend?'
'I'll see what I can do and I'll get back to you.'
Following several phone conversations over the next two days Jack booked on the early morning easy jet flight out of Liverpool and landed in Ireland approximately one hour later. He was stood outside the airport doors near to the taxi rank when two men wearing baseball caps

approached him. 'You Jack?' one of the men asked. 'That's right.' Jack acknowledged nodding his head.

One of the men waved his arm and a car sped forward and screeched to a halt in front of them. Just what I need thought Jack, low profile, like a scene from an old Sweeney movie, 'Jump in.' one of the men shouted, 'fuckinell it is a scene from an old Sweeney movie.' Jack said under his breath as he hurriedly clambered into the already moving vehicle. 'What's the rush? Jack asked.

'We've got a way to go.' One of the men replied.

'Where to.' Jack asked.

'To the bogside, Derry.' one of the men replied.

'What's Derry like?' Jack enquired.

'Derry, the man said, was built on the river Foyle, it's a city of two halves, there's a side that's a walled city and a side that isn't. The hymn, `There is a green hill far away without a city wall' was written by a resident of Derry many moons ago.'

'Very interesting.' Said Jack thinking that wasn't quite what he'd meant by his question, but interesting anyway. A while later the same man spoke again. 'This part of Derry is called the diamond and as we pass through the gate we'll be going down into the bogside, that pub over there to the right is The Rocking chair it's one of ours.' On the left Jack noticed the gable end of a house that had been painted and the message `You are now entering free Derry' was written across it in large letters, just along from there was another pub called The Bogside inn. Jack thought it best not to ask any more questions. However the talkative Irishman started to speak 'As we go up Bleases lane we pass the old army barracks, where the Brandywell brigade, the Bogside brigade, and the Creggan brigade fought the Brits, and above the Creggan is the still used army barracks Piggery ridge. The Provos headquarters was on Central Drive next to the Telstar bar and on the other side of the Telstar bar at number eleven Central Drive that was the home of Roddy Carland one of Irelands most wanted IRA gunmen in the seventies and eighties, the lads used to slip over the border to Dundalk or Bundoran, the brits couldn't touch them over there the Republic was a safe haven.' After this lecture from this unlikeliest of tourist guides there was hardly another word spoken throughout the rest of the journey and except for a necessary break at a garage to buy fuel and where Jack took the opportunity to have a quick pee and to purchase a kit kat to pamper to his hunger pains they didn't slow down. Twenty minutes after leaving the petrol station the car swung heavily to the left into a long driveway which was lined by trees and behind the trees was a timber fence, obviously to keep in the horses that were in fields on both sides of the driveway. The car that Jack was in came to a sudden stop outside a substantial and modern farmhouse, there were several men who were obviously watching the car and there were others who were doing other things but still to Jack they were also watching the car. 'Well we're here then.' The driver muttered in a heavy Irish accent. `That's bleedin obvious' thought Jack without saying anything. One of the men opened the car door and Jack got out, he followed the man into the house where he was greeted by a tall slim man who had a good head of greying hair which matched his neatly trimmed moustache, Jack thought him to be in his early fifties. 'You got here safely then.' said the softly spoken man. 'Eventually.' said Jack. 'It is a bit of a trip from the airport, would you like some refreshment, tea, coffee, something to eat?'

'I'd love a coffee.' Jack answered.

The man went out of the room and returned a minute later, where he turned to Jack holding out his hand in a gesture of friendship he said, 'I'm Sean, and Seamus has told me quite a lot about you.'

Jack taking his hand replied, 'Not to much I hope?'

'Enough.' Grinned the quiet man.

At that moment a woman entered the room, she put a tray of coffee and biscuits on the coffee

table and then she left without saying a word. Sean started to pour out the coffees 'Do you take sugar?'
'No, not for me thanks.'
'No bad habits hey Jack?' Sean smiled
'None that come to mind.' Jack smiled back.
'Help yourself to the biscuits Jack.'
'Cheers.' Jack said, as he picked up a biscuit and took a bite.
The two men sat there quietly drinking coffee and trying to get the measure of each other, they were both poker faced there was nothing being given away it was like two wild west gunfighters each waiting for the other to make a move. The old woman entering the room however broke the silence, and asking Sean if he needed anything else, he declined her kind offer and she left the room.
'Well Jack, shall we get down to business?'
'Sounds good to me.' Jack replied.
'Seamus tells me that you're interested in obtaining passports.'
'That's why I'm here.'
'How many would ya be looking for?'
'I'm not sure exactly, they're for a third party.'
'A third party, that sounds a bit ominous.'
'A foreign third party.'
'Even more intriguing, anyone we know?'
'I doubt it, they're friends of a friend.'
'A man of mystery, Jack?'
'No, not really it just sounds more complicated

than it really is.'
'Sometimes that the way it is, but I'm not so sure of that in your case.'
'Suspicious mind you've got Sean.'
'We're always suspicious here in the bogside.'
'I suppose you have to be.'
'You're not wrong Jack.'
'What the fucks that noise.' Jack blurted out.
'Ah don't worry, it's just an army chopper from Piggery ridge, they're always flying low over here.'
'Any reason for that.' Jack asked.
'Just being nosey, I think.'
'Do you get many of them over here?'
'Yeah, lots and they frighten the fucking horses half to death.'
'Can't you do anything about it?' Jack asked naively.
'It's a different world over here Jack, politics, politics and more fucking politics.'
'Well let's get back to the passport job.'
'You're very keen Jack.'
'Well it's always handy to know where you stand with the job in hand.'
'Makes sense, but there's no rush is there?'
'As long as I don't miss my flight back tonight.'
'Have you got something on?'
'Not really, just a wife and kids to get back to.'
'They'll not miss you for a night Jack and I'd like you to stay over while we get to know each other a bit better.'

'If it's no trouble.' Jack said nervously.
'I've already got a room ready for you.' Sean laughed.
Jack laughed too, but he put it down to nerves, he wasn't sure what he'd let himself in for.
'We'll go out for a drink Jack, down to our local.' Jack just nodded in agreement not quite sure what to say. Sean went to the door and shouted to some of the men outside then he came back into the room and spoke to Jack.
'Put your coat on Jack, we're off for a drink.'
With five men all squeezed into a family saloon and Jack sat in the middle on the backseat of the car, he did not feel over the moon, he thought that it was the most uncomfortable that he'd felt for quite some time. After a short while they drove past a pub he'd previously seen called The Bogside a minute later they turned into Cable Street and part way down Sean pointing his finger at a house said, 'Martin McGinnis used to live there, ...you'll have heard of him.'
'Definitely heard of him.' Jack admitted.
 A couple of minutes later the five men got out of the car and entered a pub called The Branch it was quite boisterously noisy when the men walked in, people nodded and waved to Sean and his friends it seemed like he was well known, all seemed well until Jack shouted to Sean, 'Where's the toilets in here?' The whole pub went quiet, not a soul spoke but everyone turned to look at the man who had spoken. Jack

was feeling very edgy he thought that it felt like a scene from the twilight zone, if he'd been alone he'd have been petrified. 'He's with us,' Sean's voice boomed. And with those three words the pub came alive once more and the noise worsened. Jack found his way to the loo, while he was standing at the urinal a large man rushed in and stood at the urinal next to him 'Just made it,' the man mumbled.
Jack looked across at the huge penis the man had pulled out and replied, 'Can you make me one?' The two men laughed.
Jack returned to the bar and Sean asked him what he was drinking, when Jack replied orange juice Sean started to laugh, 'You're in Ireland you can't drink orange juice,'
'And why not?'
'It's just not done, unless you've got a vodka or two in it.'
'No thanks, …do they sell hooch?'
'Yes, but that's not much better.'
'It's enough for me, a lemon one if you're buying.'
'A lemon one, Sean mumbled as he walked off smiling and shaking his head.
Sean returned a couple of minutes later, and put the bottle of hooch into Jacks hand 'A lemon one.' He grinned. Jack smiled has he took it from him.
Jack sat down amongst a bunch of men some of

who had been in the car with him earlier and others that were strangers. Jack looked around the room, and at times catching someone's suspicious eye looking back at him. There would obviously be people in there that wondered who the stranger with the English accent was, there were others who didn't want to know and then there would be the ones who thought that if he was with Sean and his men then the stranger would be okay. Jack was oblivious to the talking going on around him the heavy accented bogside voices talking at a rate of knots that made most of the chatter inaudible to him. Jack was tired, the long day, the flight, the Smokey pub, the stress, his recent injuries and the one off bottle of hooch all made for a tired Jack. Sean came over from where he'd been standing talking to two women, 'Do you fancy a woman for the night Jack?'

'You must be joking, I couldn't raise a laugh in my condition never mind anything else.' Sean laughed as he got up and walked back over to the two women, he said something to them to make them both laugh then he returned to sit next to Jack. 'What's given them the giggles?' Jack asked.

'I told them what you said about not being able to raise a laugh, they thought it was funny that's all.'

'I'm fucked, said Jack, it's been a long day.'

'If you're ready to go Jack we'll be away.'

'I'm ready when you are.' Said the knackered Jack.

Sean spoke to his men and they all proceeded to empty their beer filled glasses, it took them only seconds. They all stood up and headed for the door they waved and nodded to some of the other customers as they left. Jack and the other men were soon driving back through the bogside and on to the country lanes that led to the outskirts of Derry. 'Do you fancy a nightcap Jack?' Sean asked.

'Not unless it's one that I can put on my head.' Jack replied Sean laughed, 'You're a bit of a joker aren't you Jack?'

'Just tired mate I'm dropping on my feet.'

'I'll show you to your room.'

'Cheers.'

'Here you are Jack, Sean said as he pointed to the bedroom door, if you need anything, you only have to ask.'

'Just sleep will do fine.'

'I'll see you in the morning then.'

Jack mumbled something incoherent as he closed the bedroom door and headed for the large bed. He lay there for a few moments trying to mull over the days events in his head, it wasn't long before he was in a deep sleep only waking the next morning when he heard the sound of what was obviously a large helicopter hovering overhead. Jack forced himself out of bed, and then walking over to the window he

opened the curtains to see what was going on. He could see the huge army helicopter hovering just yards from the house then without rhyme nor reason the huge contraption turned and flew away towards Piggery ridge. Jack got dressed quickly and rushed downstairs where he bumped into Sean. 'Would you like some breakfast Jack?'
'Sure, I'm famished, what was that chopper doing outside?'
'Just being nosey as usual.'
'Nothing usual about it for me.' Jack said.
'It's like this all the time here, don't worry about it.'
'If you say so.'
Jack followed Sean into the kitchen where the little old lady from the previous day was standing by an arga cooker cooking bacon and eggs.
'Are ya feeding the masses?' Jack asked.
'It looks like it; we've got quite a few bodies about the place that need feeding,' Sean replied, another big breakfast for my friend here Mrs Boyle.' The old lady didn't reply, didn't nod or shake her head, she just carried on cooking. Very strange thought Jack very strange indeed. Sean took Jack through to the dining room where the two men sat at the table waiting for their breakfast to arrive. 'Your cook doesn't say a lot.'
'Oh, she does, but not while your around.'

'And why's that?'
'The English killed her husband and her son.'
'It wasn't me.'
'I know what you're saying, but an English man is an English man to her and she hates them all.'
'Just my fuckin luck, I hope she's not another Lizzie Borden?' 'Who the fuck's Lizzie Borden.'
'Lizzie Borden my friend is a woman who was a mass murderess.'
'Interesting?'
'She was executed for poisoning the food of her victims at a mining camp.'
Sean laughed, 'There's not much chance of her doing that here.'
'So there is some chance.'
Sean raised his eyebrows as though to think about the prospect of it and replied.
'Yes, I suppose that there's always a chance that someone could turn maverick, highly unlikely in this case but possible.'
'Go on cheer me up,' Jack said.
The room went silent as the old lady returned, she put the food on the table and left. Jack sat looking at the plate that had been put in front of him, he was pondering the Lizzie Borden theory when Sean said, 'Do you want to swap plates Jack?'
'I'd feel better.'
'Go ahead, if you want to.'

'No, its okay, I'll take a chance.'
'Living dangerous eh Jack?'
'Everyday Sean, every bleedin day.'
'A man after my own heart then.' Sean said while choking on the half of a pig that he'd just put in his mouth. Jack jumped up and slapped Sean hard on his back the big Irishman coughed the bacon back up into his hand, and then coughed some more.
'Thanks Jack.' Said Sean still clearing his throat. Sean put the bacon that was in his hand onto the side of his plate. 'Try cutting it into pieces this time, I don't want to be stood in here over your dead body trying to explain to some irate Irishmen that you've just popped your clogs eating a piece of fuckin bacon, on the other hand I could always blame Lizzie fuckin Borden.' Sean giggled a little as he thought of what the scene might have looked like.
'I'll have to be heading back to England today Sean, I've got things to do.'
'I'm sure of that Jack, but we've just got to have a meet up with my partner to see if we can come to some arrangements over the passports.
'All I need to know is the quality and the price.'
'The quality is the best, you can take my word for that, the price however, I'll have to work out with my partner.
'So when will I meet this partner of yours.'

'You already have.'
'Are you sure?'
'One hundred percent, you'll know him when you see him.'
Jack racked his brain to try to work out who it could be, but with no immediate success and Sean wasn't telling. When the two men had finished breakfast Jack dashed upstairs to take a shower having been disturbed earlier by the helicopter then being tempted to have breakfast by the smell of cooking bacon whisping through the air now was the right time to take care of personal hygiene Jack thought. On his return to the downstairs he could hear voices, he headed in the direction of where they were coming from and as Jack walked into the lounge, Scan said, 'I'd like you to meet my partner Patrick,'
'Call me Pat, the man said, as he turned around and looked into Jacks eyes. Jack looked at the man and although he couldn't place him, he knew that he'd seen him somewhere before. Pat held out his hand and Jack took it in his. After shaking hands the man said 'Don't you recognise me Jack?'
'From somewhere, but I can't place it.'
'Well next time you want someone to make a huge dick for you, have a look at their face as well.
Jack was startled. 'A huge dick,' he mumbled, then with sudden realisation, he blurted, 'You're the feller from last night at the urinals in the

Branch pub, My God how embarrassing.' said the red faced Jack.

'It was only a bit of fun, said Pat, no harm done.'

'Only to my self esteem.' Said Jack.

'It'll soon mend, said Sean, anyway it's surprising what people say after an hooch.'

The two Irishmen laughed and a second later Jack joined them. The three men sat down in the lounge to sort out the deal, Pat pulled a passport a driving licence and a birth certificate out of his coat pocket and passed them to Jack. 'They look real enough to me.' Said Jack, perusing the items carefully. 'They are real, said Pat, why fuck about with forgeries when you can get the real thing.' 'How many can you get?' asked Jack.

'How many do you want?' Pat replied.

'It's as simple as that is it?'

'As simple as that.' Came the answer.

They spent some time discussing prices and the possibilities of other deals that may or may not reach fruition. Pat got up to leave, 'It's been nice meeting you Jack, and whatever happens keep in touch.' Pat left the house and the door closed heavily behind him.

'He must like you Jack.' Said Sean.

'Why's that?'

'Because he doesn't often ask people, especially strangers to keep in touch.

'Strangers, Jack retorted, after last night we're

practically lovers.' The two men laughed. After the reappearance of Mrs Boyle and some chit chat with Sean over a coffee Jack asked Sean if he could find out the flight times for him, so that he could make his way home. He returned a couple of minutes later and said, 'There's a flight in just under three hours and there's plenty of seats, I'll get one my lads to take you, do you need anything more before you go?'
'No, I'm fine.' Jack replied.
Five hours later Jack was turning into the driveway of his own house, pleased to be home and thankful that he'd be sleeping in his own bed that very night.

Chapter Three

It was almost twelve o'clock the next day when Jack surfaced from his warm and comfortable bed. 'Would you like some tea hon?' Sandra asked, as Jack trundled down the stairs in his dressing gown. 'Yes please, I'd love one, I'm just running the bath.'
'It's late you know?'
'I know, but I was just too knackered to get up, the last couple of days have worn me away.'
'I think the last couple of years have worn you away darling.'
'You're probably right.'
Jack flopped himself down on his large leather sofa while Sandra disappeared into the kitchen to make some tea. Soon Sandra returned with a piping hot brew to replenish Jacks energy levels, he always felt better after he'd had a cup of hot tea it gave him a kick-start to the day. It wasn't long before he was dashing back upstairs to make sure his bath wasn't overflowing, he stripped of his bathrobe, then put one foot in the half filled bath, he turned off the taps, he knew that his body weight would force the water the rest of the way up, it was a bit hot but he still lowered himself into the welcoming water and

disappeared up to his neck in bubbles. After a few minutes of laying there lifeless, he almost fell back to sleep, it was only the fact that Sandra had entered the bathroom noisily that had caused him to open his eyes. 'Still tired honey,' she asked.
'I didn't think that I was until I got in here, it's sapped all my energy at least what I had left.'
'What a waste,' she giggled.
Jack pushed his feet against the bottom end of the bath causing himself to sit up, Sandra then sat on the edge of the bath and picking up a sponge she started to wash his shoulders gently.
'Still tired honey,' she whispered.
'I'm waking up again now.'
Sandra leaned forward to kiss Jack on the forehead and as she did, Jack gripped the unsuspecting Sandra and pulled her fully dressed into the bath causing the bath to overflow onto the bathroom floor. 'Jack, the startled Sandra screamed, you'll ruin the bathroom.'
'I'll worry about that later, are you wet dear?'
'Just a bit.'
'We'd better get you out of these wet clothes then.'
She looked at him and grinned, she leaned forward and kissed him passionately on the lips, Jack slipped his tongue in and out of her mouth, his hands were all over her firm soap soaked body, she felt the tightness of her bra become

loose as Jacks hand slipped under her top and released her huge breasts from the shackles that had encaged them, he then slipped her flimsy now see through soaking top off over her head and the bra straps underneath fell off her arms leaving her breasts exposed as she sat straddled above him the water splashing about around them, but they were oblivious to all but passion at this stage, she could feel Jacks erect penis pressing against her body, Jack lifted her skirt above her hips then slipping his hand into the front side of her wet knickers he pulled them to one side, at the same time using his other hand and with some help from Sandra he entered her body as she let out a loud pleasurable scream, Jack was thrusting upwards towards Sandra as she was riding up and down on his huge erection, she then started to get more excited, causing Jack to feel a throbbing deep in his loins the pair were thrusting together faster and faster until with screams from both of them they collapsed into each others arms breathless and exhausted. After a couple of minutes Sandra helped Jack to get out of the bath and took him back to bed where they stayed for most of the afternoon. The following day Jack rang Pete and told him to make arrangements for a meeting with the Turk, without Jack saying anything on the phone Pete knew it was going to be a deal about passports. Pete set up the meeting for the following day. It was almost ten o'clock when

Jack pulled up outside Pete's house and beeped the horn briefly to let Pete know that he was there, Pete struggled out of his front door still trying to put his clothes on. 'Late night Pete?' Jack smiled.
'Just a bit, the Mrs you know gotta keep her happy.'
'Suppose so pal.' Jack said thoughtfully.
They were half way to Leicester on the Motorway when Pete decided that he was hungry having had no breakfast; he was trying to coax Jack into stopping at one of the service stations so that he could grab some munchies.
'A night on the pot Pete.'
'Just a little spliff or two Jack, nothing heavy.'
'You'll be fuckin heavy if ya eat all this food that ya keep talking about.'
'Funny, I don't think.'
'No need to start sulking, we'll pull off at the next services, I need some fuel anyway.'
'Cheers.'
It wasn't long before Jack, and the now well-fed Pete arrived outside the Turks house. Jack as per normal for him sat in the car while the ever overworked Pete made his way to the Turks door, he knocked and waited for a couple of minutes, he was just about to knock again when the door opened, it was the little Turk himself, the two men spoke then Pete turned to where Jack was sat in the car and waved for him to come to the house. Jack

clambered out of the car and marched briskly to the door of the Turks house where the skeletal man greeted him. The Turk went into the house and the two men followed him, this time they went into a different room not quite as shabby as the first room they'd sat in, but still not to a standard of hygiene that Jack would have preferred, the musky smell was very strong and extremely noticeable to Jacks nostrils and he was sure that even the unobservant Pete had at least noticed this pungent odour. 'Would you like some tea?' the Turk asked politely.
'No,' both men barked at the same time, 'We've just had some on the Motorway.' Pete mumbled. 'Okay, very good, down to business then.'
Jack then took from the inside pocket of his Jacket a brown A5 size envelope slightly folded and passed it to Pete who was sat somewhere between the two men, Pete in turn passed it to the Turk. The Turk slowly but surely unfolded the brown package and opened the envelope, taking from it a passport, a driving license and birth certificate all brand new all perfect and all blank. 'These are very good.' said the Turk. 'They should be,' demanded Jack, they're all real.'
'Real,' muttered the Turk.
'They're definitely real, there's no forgeries,

and even if they were forgeries they'd still be good enough for most jobs.'

'They look good enough to me, but I'll need to show them to someone, will it be all right if I keep hold of these for a few days, the other thing that I need to know about is the price.' Jack and the Turk talked for a while before Jack hit him with a price, the Turk seemed happy enough, Pete seemed bewildered, the first time he'd seen the documents was when the Turk opened the envelope so he was clueless about the whole deal, but he wasn't to worried; he always knew that when Jack put a price on anything there was always a shilling or two in it for him in there somewhere. Having discussed the business with the Turk and got the deal at least moving in the right direction, Jack and Pete made their excuses and left before they got offered any more tea. 'What was that tea like?' Jack asked has they drove away from the Turks house. 'What tea?' Pete asked.

'The tea you had at the Turks, the last time we came.'

'It was fuckin orrible.'

'Horrible, you drank most of it?'

'I didn't want him to think that I was being funny.'

'Being funny, your face was twisted like you'd swallowed a lemon.' Jack chortled.

'It wasn't funny, it tasted like curdled

goats milk.'
'Oh you've tasted that have you?'
'No, but you know what I mean.'
'A bit rough then.'
'I was ill for days.'
'Was ya now?' Jack asked laughing lightly, expecting no answer and getting none. Two days later early in the morning and Jack was awoken by his mobile phone playing some mad tune that his kids had put on it. Jack spoke into the tiny hole in the little box
'Hello, anybody there?' Jack mumbled.
'Is that you Jack?'
'Yeah, who's that?'
'It's me Angel.'
'Right, what's happening?'
'I've got some movement on that matter that we discussed, can we meet?'
'Sure, I'll ring you back shortly.' Jack had a quick shower then got into his car and headed for Angels house, ringing him from his mobile en route to let him know that he was on his way. Angel seemed really excited about the deal, Jack had hardly got through his front door when the Irishman went into a tirade of information he was speaking very fast his face was glowing red Jack thought that he must be on drugs. 'Whoa, said Jack, Slow down.'
'Right, right, come through and take a seat.' Jack followed Angel into a room he called his office, and sat down on the chesterfield settee.

Angel having taken a minute or two to regain his breath, explained to Jack that he could definitely put his end of the deal together, it was just a matter now of whether the other people involved could do their part. Jack assured him that everyone else would be able to do his or her part as long as he could organise his bit, Angel guaranteed his end and Jack said that he would go and put all the pieces together to complete the plan and then hopefully they could all make some money. Jack left Angels house and went to meet Pete 'It looks like the cig job is going to come off we've got someone to sort half of it.'
'Good, I've had a call off the Turk, he wants ten passports for a starter, and if they do the job he reckons he'll be wanting a lot more.'
'He'll be wanting a lot more then.' Jack responded.
'That good eh Jack.'
'Excellent, Pete.'
'We might earn a shilling or two then eh Jack.'
'We might at that Pete, we might at that.' Jack said repeating himself; 'I'm off Pete I'll catch up with you later.'
'Okay Jack, I'll be at home.'
The two men parted company. Jack also headed home to see his beloved Sandra. The following evening after several phone calls during the day Jack took a flight to Belfast where he was once again met by Sean's men who took him on another wild journey

through the bogside and down some narrow country lanes to Sean's house. As they pulled into Sean's driveway the men could hear the clattering noise of the helicopter overhead, they all looked up at the menacing object hovering over the trees that lined the driveway. 'Not again.' Jack snapped.
'Don't worry it's about ten times a day at the moment.'
'Why's that asked Jack?'
'We'd all like to know the answer to that one, we're to close to piggery ridge that's for sure.' The car had by now pulled up outside the front door of Sean's house, one of the men standing there opened the car door to let Jack out, the loudness of the helicopters vast rotary blades was almost deafening, none of the men were taking any notice of this huge monstrosity that hovered above them, yet it still hung there floating like a bird of prey waiting to attack, to the uninitiated member like Jack it was all very unnerving, but for the people who had grown up and lived in this war zone it was an everyday occurrence. As Jack walked towards the main door he heard a noise, he turned and looked up at the helicopter it was hovering low and he could see that someone was taking photographs, he immediately turned his face away and rushed into the house through the now open door. Sean was standing just inside the hallway and as the

two men greeted each other they heard the engine of the chopper accelerate loudly and as they looked out of the open doorway they watched as the flying tank turned and raced away towards piggery ridge. 'It was a grand welcome for you Jack, we don't bring the chopper out for everyone.' Sean laughed.
'I'm getting paranoid, I think that fucking contraption is following me.'
'Maybe it's you Jack, and I thought it was us they keep looking at.'
'What I'm worried about is that they might be looking at both of us.'
'They'll certainly be interested in who you are if they've just nicked your picture.'
'I wish I hadn't looked up.'
'To late wishing now, fuckem anyway they're just a load of nosey bastards.'
'I'm hoping you know what you're doing?'
'We do, but we like to play a few games with them, keep them on their toes.'
'It looks like they were more than on their toes, it only takes one nutter in that chopper and the jobs fucked.'
'Take no notice Jack, it's all a game.'
'Well I'll just be a spectator in this one.'
'A wise move Jack but not easy when you're playing on the pitch.'
'This is just a business deal.'
'They won't see it like that.'
'Now ya tell me.'

'Forget it Jack, let's get down to business.'
Sean said as he led Jack through to the lounge. Jack explained to Sean about the deal for the ten passports with orders of many more to come, Sean offered to get the passports for Jack the next day but Jack had not brought the necessary photographs with him nor did he fancy the idea of carrying ten passports with him back to England, Jack arranged to send a man with the cash to pay for the passports, the same man would bring the ten photographs to Ireland, and then hang around until they were ready before returning to England with the goods. 'Sounds simple enough to me, I'll ring you as soon as I get the photos.'

'Okay Jack, we'll leave it at that, you'll not get a flight back tonight, we might as well nip down to the branch for a Guinness or two or in your case a lemon hooch.'

'If I can't get a flight tonight that's okay, but I'll ring and try anyway.' Jack rang and couldn't get a flight, so he booked one for early the next morning. 'Will anyone be awake at five in the morning?' Jack asked.

'I doubt it.' Said Sean, but if not we'll organise you a taxi.'

'A taxi, around here.' Declared Jack.

'It's not from around here, but a friend of mine runs a firm in the city, I'll have a word.'

'Cheers.' Jack said, not quite sure if he was happy or not or whether or not he'd be catching the early flight. Sean called his men together and two carloads of men headed for the Branch pub. Three hours at the pub soon flew by and the now merry if not drunken men were heading home to Sean's house. Once they arrived at Sean's, Jack said that he had to get his head down, as he had to be up early the next morning, the men said their goodbyes and Jack retired to bed. When Sean arose at ten o'clock the next morning Jack was already back at home in England. After having a shower and getting changed Jack went to Pete's house. 'On your own again Pete?'

'Yeah, she's always popping out somewhere or other, it gives me some peace, some time to sit and ponder.'

'The meaning of life,' Jack butted in.

'No, nothing so deep, usually only where the next shilling is coming from.

'I know the feeling, anyway talking of a shilling or two I've got a job for you.'

'This sounds a bit ominous.'

'It's nothing difficult, I want you to take some cash and some passport photos to Ireland where you'll meet some people who will relieve you of the said cash and photos, they will then arrange to meet you later or the next day at your hotel where they will return the photos to you but by then they will be attached to the necessary passports, did you follow all that?'

'Sort of.'

Jack then took out his mobile phone and began to make the necessary arrangements after a few minutes he turned to Pete and said, 'That's sorted then, you'll fly out in the morning.'
'What if I get a tug on the way back with all them passports?'
'You won't.'
'Why not?'
'Because you won't have any passports on you, once these Irish guys have given you the passports I want you to go down to the post office and post them back to ten different addresses, which I'll give to you later, are you with the show so far?'
'Yeah, I've got it.'
'Good man, right, I'm off for now, I'll see you later.'
Jack let himself out of Pete's house and headed for Sandra's car, which he'd borrowed earlier.
The next day the extremely terrified Pete found himself not only in Ireland but sat in the back of a car squashed between two large men, they pulled onto a hotel car park
'Have you got the money?' one of the men asked as the car ground to a halt. Pete had a feeling of impending doom, he hesitated, then slightly stuttering he said 'It, it, it's in the blue bag that you put in the boot.'
One of the men got out and went to the boot of the car, returning a few seconds later with two

bags the black one he threw to Pete, 'Your clothes in that one are they'
'Yeah.' said the nodding Pete.
'Right, there's plenty of room in this hotel, we'll ring you when the job's sorted out.'
'That'll be fine.' Pete mumbled as he clambered out of the car, relieved to be still in one piece. Jack Dunkerley knows some extremely dodgy characters Pete thought to himself as he walked into the foyer of the hotel. Back in England Jack was moving ahead with his plan to organise a few wagon loads of cigarettes, he had been in touch with Angel who confirmed that his end was now one hundred percent water tight, and also with Roger to make sure that he was not only still up for it but that he also was ready to go at short notice, Jack now satisfied that everyone was ready, having that in mind Jack got in touch with Seamus who in turn got in touch with his Gibraltan friends with a view to them placing a few orders for cigarettes from a couple of cigarette companies in England. Jack was quite pleased that things were starting to move along unlike Pete who was lying on the bed in his hotel room and getting the strange idea in his head that he'd been robbed and dumped in Ireland by some very large men that he was unlikely ever to see again. Pete leaned over off the bed and picked his Jacket off the bedside chair, taking his mobile phone from the inside pocket he dialled his home number to

ring his wife, there was no answer. 'Out again.' Pete mumbled to himself.' He decided to go out to buy some cigs and maybe grab a quick beer. He returned an hour later to find that he'd missed three calls none of which registered their own number on his phone, somewhat perplexed, Pete phoned Jack.

'I've not phoned you Pete, it must be the Irish mob, don't worry about it they'll ring you back when they're ready.'

'Okay, I'll get my head down, and see what happens in the morning.'

'Yeah, you do that Pete.' They said their goodbyes and the phones were turned off. Before retiring for the night Pete rang home once more to speak to his wife, his house phone rang for what seemed like a long time to Pete, he switched off the phone, mumbling to himself out loud 'She's not in again, very odd.' The tired Pete stripped off and climbed naked into the huge inviting bed and in no time at all he had drifted off into the land of nod. Eleven o'clock the following morning the still asleep Pete was woken by someone shaking his arm, in a sleepy panic Pete sat bolt upright trying to adjust his eyes to what was going on around him. 'What's up, what's up?' he kept asking. 'Nothing is up,' said one of the three men standing around his bed, 'We tried to ring you last night and again this morning, and when we got no answer we thought we'd better come and see if you were alright.'

'I'm okay, said Pete, I went out last night for a while and I forgot to take the phone with me, and as you can see I've overslept this morning.'

'Well as long as you're okay, there's your passports.' The man said has he threw a brown package onto the bed.

'Cheers.' Pete squeaked, then coughing to clear his throat.

Pete jumped out of bed as soon as the three men had left the room, he was in a rush to get his job done so that he could get a flight and head for home. Pete showered, got dressed and then lighting a cigarette as he headed for the post office carrying his package. 'I can't believe my fuckin luck.' Pete shouted down the phone to Jack. 'What's up?'

'What's up, what's fuckin up? I'll tell you what's up the only day of the fuckin week that the post office shuts for half a day, and I fuckinwell oversleep.'

'Not having a good day then Pete.' Jack remarked.

'That's the understatement of the year Jack, I couldn't get any answer at home last night, so I had an early night not expecting to oversleep, then I wake up this morning with three big Paddy's in the room, one of them trying to rip my arm out of the fuckin socket, then I struggle to find the main Post office only to find that it

had shut ten minutes before I fucking well got there.'
'Another night in Paradise then Pete?'
'Paradise, there's soldiers and police driving round in fuckin tanks.'
'Well it is a bit of a war zone Pete.'
'Thanks mate, I needed a bit of cheering up.'
'Do you want me to call at your house to see if there's anything wrong with your phone?'
'No, I'll sort it myself Jack, but thanks anyway, I'll have to get back to the hotel to let them know that I'm staying another night.'
'Okay Pete, keep in touch.'
'Hopefully I'll see you tomorrow.'
'You might if your luck changes.'
'Don't be saying that Jack I'm having nightmares as it is.' 'Give me a ring tomorrow Pete, when you're sorted.'
'If I get sorted.'
'You will, I've got faith in you.'
'That's one of us.' Pete quipped as the phone went dead. Pete returned to the hotel and booked in for another night, he went to his room and lay on the bed for a while, and then taking out his mobile phone he rang his house.
'Oh, you are alive then!' Pete growled as his wife answered the phone. 'Why what's up?'
'What's up, I've been trying to get hold of you since yesterday.'

'Well the phones been on, and I've not been out, maybe I was asleep.'
'A bit coincidental that every time I rang, you were asleep.'
'Maybe there's something wrong with the phone!'
'Well it's working now!'
'I don't know what the problem is but I've not heard it ring until now.'
'Maybe it's something to do with this International dialling.' Said Pete disregarding his previous thoughts. Pete and Jane chatted for a while, Pete said that he'd be home the next day and she said that she'd be waiting for him, he promised that he would take her out for a meal the next evening and she sounded pleased, they were about to say their goodbyes when Pete's phone cut off, the battery had gone flat. 'Bastard,' Pete shouted to an empty room, 'no fuckin charger with me either.' Pete decided to go downstairs to the bar for some liquid refreshment, he was tempted to use one of the public phones to ring Jane but he remembered what Jack had told him about the public phones in Ireland. The next morning Pete was on an early flight and he was back in England in time for breakfast. He turned the key in the lock of his front door and opened it quietly in case Jane was asleep, she was in bed rolled up into a ball underneath their king size duvet, Pete stripped off and slipped into the bed with her, she was

half awake but seemed a bit on edge when she realised that Pete was there. Pete took note of this but said nothing has he didn't want to be the cause of another argument between the two of them; maybe it's women's problems he thought. Later in the day Pete rang Jack to let him know that he was back, they arranged to meet for some dinner at six o'clock in the Mucky Duck where they would discuss recent events if the pub was quiet, which it usually was at that time in the dining area. Pete now armed with a fully charged battery on his phone was ready for some action or so he thought until his phone rang into life causing him to have a serious fright. Pete mumbled into the phone only a few words,

'Yes, who, I've got them, I'll ask him, okay bye.'

It was nearly six thirty when the last of the afternoons tail enders finally left the dining area of the Mucky Duck; at last the two men could talk about business instead of the bollocks that they'd had to talk about while they were being overheard by other diners.

'The fucking worlds gone mad Jack!'

'Yeah, I know,'

'All these deals we're involved in, don't you think we're taking too much on?'

'No, why do you?'

'It's a lot of graft Jack, plus the work we're already doing.'

'We don't know how much will come to fruition, so we've got to keep our options open.'

'Suppose so, bye the way the Turk rang me today.'

'He's on the ball, the post won't arrive til at least tomorrow.'

'When I told him it was sorted, he asked me if you could shift some paintings for him.' 'What did you say?'

'I said I'd see.'

'What paintings are they?'

'I didn't ask.'

'Probably just as well on the phone, you'll have to set up a meet.' 'Right, but that means another trip to Leicester.'

'You're right but you'd have to go in any case to take the passports to him; anyway it's better than bringing him and his mob up here and attracting some unnecessary attention from the fucking odd-lot.'

'You've got a point Jack.'

'Yeah, I know, let's order some food I'm starving it's been a long day.' 'You can say that again.' Pete agreed.

'I'm starving it's been a long day.'

'Fucking comedian now are you Jack?'

'No sense of humour some people.' Jack said to the almost empty room.

The two men sat around chatting away about

all the plans they had, they mulled over the different names and reasons why someone would want to shoot Jack. They even tried to solve the problems of the world in the two and a half hours that they'd sat there since the room had emptied. They got up to leave. 'Tomorrows another day.' Said Jack stating the obvious. The passports didn't arrive the next day as expected so Jack decided to postpone his trip to Leicester until they'd arrived at the addresses to which he'd had them sent, that way he wouldn't be going on any journeys, where he'd be driving hundreds of miles, just to have a chat to someone and then either him or Pete having to do the same journey the next day just to deliver the passports. So the following day when the passports finally arrived and Pete had been to all the addresses to collect them he called to collect Jack from The Highwayman where they'd arranged to meet, Pete walked into the bar and shouted to Jack 'Are you ready Jack?' 'Yeah, I'm coming.' He shouted back has he got up from the table where he'd been sat talking to two men. Jack and Pete walked along the short road towards the car park then just as they got to the edge of the car park a dark saloon car started to drive towards the exit, as it got along side them Jack noticed something unusual, he grabbed Pete and threw himself and Pete onto the floor in one swift movement, at that moment Jack heard a loud bang, a screaming engine and

the screech of tyres as the saloon car sped away towards the main road, Jack grabbed hold of the fence of the children's play area next to where he and Pete had been lay on the damp floor, Jack used the fence to pull himself up to his feet, Pete got up off the floor saying 'What the fuck was all that about.' 'I don't know Pete, but it wasn't trick or treat, was it?' Pete headed for the car and Jack hobbled after him, they got in swiftly and drove across the car park. 'Should I chase after them Jack?'
'Should you fuck! They'll be well gone by now, and what we going to do if we catch them, they've got a fucking gun and we've got two packets of crisps and a flask of tea.'
'You're right Jack, so what now?'
'Motorway Pete, and head for Leicester.'
Pete turned right as he pulled away from the Highwayman and drove along Manchester road towards the Motorway junction, just before they got to the traffic island that leads onto the Motorway, Jack shouted, 'Pull into this lay-by Pete, my leg's stinging like fuck.' Pete pulled into the lay-by and Jack opened the car door and stuck his leg out, he reached down to where his leg was hurting, he felt that it was soaking wet, he squeezed his hurting calf muscle and then on lifting his hand he could see that it was covered in blood Jack got out of the car and hobbled around for a while, he was losing the feeling in his leg.

'They must have got you Jack.' Pete mumbled.
'I've gathered that Pete.' Jack snapped.
'What the fuck are we going to do now, you'll have to go to the hospital the way that fucking legs leaking.'
'You're right Pete, all the way round this island back towards the hozzy, you'll have to fuck off when we get there in case the odd-lot turn up and find you in possession of several dodgy passports.'
'Okay,' what do you want me to do then?'
'Then my friend I want you to carry on the journey to Leicester.' 'What about them paintings?'
'Just find out what they are and who they're by and don't forget to find out the price.'
Pete and his wounded friend pulled onto the hospital car park. 'Where do you want me to drop you Jack?'
'Somewhere close enough to the door, but far enough away so that you can get away without being seen to easy.'
'I'll just drive past and go round the corner, you'll only have to walk back a few yards.'
'That'll be fine Pete.'
Jack waited until Pete had driven off before he made his way to the automatic doors that led to the casualty department. Jack was soon taken through to the nursing bay; he jumped the queue because of the amount of blood he was losing. There was a doctor there very quickly; the

doctor and nurse together spent quite some time attending to Jack's wounds. The doctor went from the nursing bay and the nurse was left to finish off bandaging Jack's wounds. The doctor in the presence of the nurse had asked Jack about how the injuries had come about, Jack had replied that he didn't know, and the doctor had left it at that. It was only when the nurse pulled back the curtain on Jack's bay at the end of his treatment that he realised that there were two faces there that he knew. 'Well Dunkerley,' one of them said, 'What's happened this time?'
'I've no idea,' Jack said, 'I was just walking along the road when I felt a wetness on my leg, knowing that I'd not just had an orgasm, I was suspicious, I put my hand on my leg and when I looked at my hand I could see blood so I thought I'd better come here to the hospital to see if they could fix it, which they did.'
'Still a funny bastard eh Dunkerley? 'The doctor says you've got shotgun wounds.'
'Does he now?'
'He does.'
'Well I don't know how he's come to that conclusion.' 'Because he's a doctor and he's seen it all before.'
'All eh?'
'Listen Dunkerley, for some reason there's someone out there trying to kill you and we want to know who it is?'
'If that was right, I'd want to know as well.'

'You're hiding something Dunkerley, we'll get to the bottom of this.' The older now brightly red-faced detective shouted almost screaming himself into frenzy. The younger detective pulled his arm and the two Detectives stormed out of the building. Jack said nothing more; he just stared at the two men as they left. He smiled Jack found a taxi for himself outside the casualty department, on arriving home, Sandra said, 'I thought you wouldn't be back til late.'

'There's been a change of plan, Pete's gone on his own.' 'So you can spend some time with me,' she laughed.

'Why ever not?' Jack declared as he hobbled over to his chair.

'What have you done to your leg Jack?' Sandra asked.

'Nothing much, I got it caught on some jagged metal that was sticking out on Pete's old banger.'

'Trust you, as though you're not having enough problems.'

'I'll just put my feet up, any chance of a brew?'
 'Another skive is it, bad leg
 can't make it to the kitchen.'
 She laughed. 'I'm not
 skiving, my legs in agony.'
 'You'll have to go to the hospital if it's that bad.'
 'Maybe later.'

'Okay, you've got the sympathy vote, I'll make some tea.' 'You are so kind darling.' Jack said as he blew her a kiss. 'Stop creeping Jack, I'm onto you.'
'You wish.' He laughed.
A few hours later Pete arrived at Jack's house, Sandra opened the door to him. 'Is Jack in?'
'He's asleep in his chair, I'll wake him it's time he was up now anyway or he won't sleep tonight.'
'He's probably worn away with all the blood that he lost.' 'Was it a lot?'
'It seemed to be, but you know Jack?'
'Yes, I know what he's like.'
'He told you what happened then.'
'Yes, but accidents do happen.'
'You're taking it in good spirits Sandra.'
'Well we can't get hysterical over every little mishap can we.' She said not wanting to upset Pete over the state of his car.
'Mishap, I could probably think of a better word.'
'You probably could Pete.' She said has she shook Jacks arm until his eyes opened. 'What time is it?' he asked groggily.
'It's nearly eight o'clock.' Sandra answered has she pointed at the clock on the mantelpiece, 'Pete's here.'
'Right I'm awake, I'm awake.' Mumbled Jack.

Sandra walked off towards the kitchen but before she got to the door, she heard Pete say to Jack, 'Who was that who tried to murder us today?' 'Murder you,' Sandra screamed, walking back towards the two men 'What are you talking about?'

'Fuckinell Pete.' Jack groaned.

'I thought you'd told her, and Sandra said that she knew.'

'That's because I thought that I did, what's going on Jack?' snapped the angry Sandra. Between Jack and Pete they explained to Sandra roughly what had happened at the Highwayman. She was not impressed that Jack had kept it from her but she could understand that he did not want to worry her anymore than necessary. Sandra made some tea while Jack and Pete discussed the passports and the Turk, Pete also mentioned a couple of paintings that he'd wrote the names down of that the Turk wanted to shift, but he'd left the paper at home in his other Jacket. Jack wasn't to bothered firstly as he didn't know the slightest thing about paintings and secondly and more importantly he wanted to know who was trying to kill him. Jack, Sandra, and Pete sat around for quite some time trying to work out what it was all about, but couldn't come up with an answer to this most serious of problems.

Sandra said, 'Who knew that you were going to be at the Highwayman Jack?'

'Only Pete.' Jack said while staring at Pete.
'Hang on a minute Jack, it's nothing to do with me.' 'I didn't say that it was, did I?'
'I know what you're saying Jack, but I'm never sure what you're thinking.' 'What I'm thinking Pete is that you have got nothing to do with this.' 'I'm glad that you think that way Jack.'
'You'd be the last person on the list mate, it would the worst case of chopping off the hand that feeds you in the history of man.'
'You're not wrong Jack, if it wasn't for our wheeling and dealing I'd be on the fuckin dole living on beans on toast and Spam butties.'
'Well there you go, no point in you having me bumped off then.' Said Jack half grinning.
'Who else knew that you were going to the Highwayman?' Sandra asked slowly but surely.
'No one.' Jack replied.
'Are you sure Jack?'
'Positive.'
'What about you Pete, did you tell anyone?'
'No,' he said then thinking on he said, 'Only my Mrs, but she'd have no reason to .... ' his words drifted away endless.
'No, she wouldn't,' said Jack so lets try to find the real culprit, and as we've come to a brick wall for now, I'm tired and I'm throwing my hand in for the night.' 'Me too Jack, I'm

bushed.'

'Okay Pete, I'll see you tomorrow.'

Pete said his goodbyes to Jack and Sandra as he walked towards their front door, he turned and waved as he let himself out.'

'Do you believe that he had nothing to do with it Jack?' Sandra demanded, Pete might be Jack's mate, but Jack was her husband and when it came to protecting him she trusted no one. 'He's one hundred percent San, we've been through wars together me and Pete.' 'It's just very strange Jack, all these things going on, and no one putting their face to it. 'Someone will San, someone will.' Jack struggled to take his trousers off which exposed his bandaged leg. 'It doesn't look like nothing to me Jack!' 'Just a scratch hon.'

'Hmmm!' Sandra mused has she emptied Jacks trouser pockets.' 'What are you doing?' Jack asked.

'Throwing these away.' Sandra replied, holding his torn and bloodstained trousers up for him to see. 'Don't suppose they're much use now.' Jack moaned. 'Not a lot.' She said has she walked out of the room, carrying the tattered material with her. The tired Jack limped across the lounge towards the stairs as Sandra returned from the Garbage bin in time to help him to climb the stairway to their bedroom.

The following day when Pete returned, Jack was still in bed, 'He's probably still tired out

from yesterday.' Sandra said.
' I'll call back later.' Pete said.
'I'm awake,' Jacks voice boomed from the top of the stairs, 'Come in Pete, we've got things to do.'
'I'm already in Jack.'
Jack hobbled down the stairs; his now battered leg throbbing has blood pumped through the injured part of his calf muscle. Jack had refused to stay in the hospital so he was unlikely to get any sympathy there, but what could they do anyway? He might as well be in discomfort at home as be in discomfort and bored at the hospital he thought as he limped across the room to his armchair. 'Would you like some breakfast Jack?' Sandra asked. 'I could eat an horse.' Jack replied.
'One horse, coming up,' Sandra grinned, 'would you like some Pete?'
'Wouldn't say no, I'm a bit peckish.'
'Two horses coming up.' She laughed as she disappeared into the kitchen. 'Right Jack, Pete started, I've got this list off the Turk.' 'List.' Jack mumbled.
'Yeah, a list of goodies, that the Turk can get his hands on, and he wants to know if we can shift it on.'
Pete went on to read out a list of goodies that the Turk said he could get his hands on; the list captured Jacks imagination, multi-million dollar paintings, gold coins and other treasures that

had been secreted away, all relics of the now obsolete Ottoman Empire. Jacks imagination was alight; the fuse had been lit with this phenomenal information his brain was burning with a multitude of ideas, all vying for poll position. But all he could manage to say to Pete was 'Fuckinell.'
'No other comments Jack?
'If this guy is for real, we could be onto something mega.'
'Mega is definitely a word that might cover it.' Pete laughed.
'What are you two laughing at?' Sandra asked as she returned from the kitchen carrying two cups.
'Mega.' Jack replied, laughing.
Sandra put the two cups of tea down, 'Can't see anything funny about the word mega.'
She moaned has she walked back to the kitchen shaking her head. 'Things might be looking up then Pete!' Jack grinned.
'Except for having to dodge the odd bullet here and there.'
'Well that does tend to take the fun out of the job a bit.' Jack said thoughtfully. 'That may well be a bit of an understatement Jack.'
'Sorry, I was miles away then.'
'Penny for your thoughts Jack?'
'I was just thinking about who it could be taking pot shots at us and why, I haven't got an answer and that's enough to drive me mad.'

'It drives me mad too Jack, I've wracked my brain, the same names and faces come up time and time again but then nothing, no motive, not one fuckin reason for this sort of grief.'
'I know Pete, I've been around the houses too mate; but always the same answer, a fuckin big zero.'
'Mad innit?' Pete blurted.
'Pete,' Jack said slowly, 'The whole fucking worlds gone mad.'

Chapter four

It was a couple of weeks before Jack felt well enough to travel down to Leicester to meet the Turk and when he got there the Turk seemed very pleased to see him. 'Nice to see that you are back on your feet Jack, Pete told me that you've been ill.' 'Just a bad dose of flu.' Jack lied.

'Have you found any buyers for the items that I told Pete about?' He asked.

'Not yet, I want to make sure that you can get these goods before I get involved or I'm going to be left looking stupid.'

'Everything and more Jack.'

'It seems a lot of stuff for one man to be in possession of?' 'It makes sense for you to be cynical, but I've got the items.' 'You also said and more.'

'Don't miss much do you Jack?'

'Not when there's a shilling involved.'

'The main item is the Torah.'

'The Torah.' Jack repeated.

'Yes, it's the five original scriptures, they are written on animal skin, it's on a huge scroll thirty metres long, it is a very important piece.'

'What's it worth?' Jack asked.

'It's a priceless piece but the asking price

from my people is twenty million dollars.'
'Twenty million fuckin dollars.' Jack heard
himself shouting. 'At that price it's for
nothing.' The Turk said calmly.
'And if I find a buyer, what would I be paid?'
Jack enquired. 'Half a million sterling.'
'Worth having a go then.' Jack smiled.
'If you've got the connections it will be an easy
payday for you Jack.'
'It's whether they're interested.' Jack ad-libbed
not having a clue who he was going to approach
or even if there was anyone. Having spent over
an hour in the company of the Turk, Jack had
found out many things that could be to his
advantage, he mulled over many of these
possibilities as he drove home. Some hours later
after he'd been home and had his tea with
Sandra he once again left his house and went to
meet Pete. He explained to Pete about the
Torah, but Pete didn't grasp the historical
importance of this piece. 'The problem that I
see, said Jack, is that if there are many
governments around the world looking for it,
why haven't they found it?'
'Maybe it doesn't exist?' Pete replied.
'It must, but the problem that we have, is that
we can't go asking about it just in case we
attract the wrong sort of interest.'
'What do you call the wrong sort of attention?'
'Any attention is the wrong sort, but if it
does exist and it's part of the Jewish heritage

then we'll have Mosad or the like hunting us down and they are a very serious mob.'
'It's not going to get that heavy is it Jack?'
'I hope not pal, we don't need that sort of shit.'
'I don't know what it is and I'm scared shitless already.' 'Can't blame ya Pete, it's heavy shit.
'Yeah, let's change the subject.'
'Good idea, maybe nothing will come of it anyway.'
'You're probably right Jack, we've probably spent more on fuel, back and too, to the Turks house than we'll ever make on any of his deals.'
'Lets hope not Pete, I'm not in this for health reasons.' 'It's my health, I'm worried about Jack.'
'Mine too Pete, but no dosh no eat, and no eat also leads to bad health.'
'Eating's not one of my worries Jack, a fuckin bullet in the napper is more scary, and that does not cheer me up at all.'
'Fuckinell Pete we've only talked about it and your crappin yourself already, it might never fuckin happen.'
'It's not the `never' bit that frightens me, it's the `might never' bit that fuckin terrifies me.
'Well Pete if it all goes wrong, I hope that you're in heaven a long time before the devil knows that you're dead.'
'Very reassuring Jack, I must say.' Said the pale looking Pete.

Just after that morbid conversation took place
the two men parted company agreeing to
meet up at the Mucky Duck the following day
for lunch. Jack went home to see Sandra and
his children, while Pete headed home to see
his beloved Jane.
'One of us will have to go to Ireland to have a
word with Scan about these treasures that
we've come across.'
'One of us Jack, when you say one of us, you
usually mean me.' 'Well I've got a bad leg Pete.'
'Fuckin marvellous, I knew that I shouldn't have
come today.' 'Cheer up, it's not the end of the
world.'
'It feels like it Jack, them big paddy's are a
law to themselves, I could go missing over
there and no one would ever find me.'
'Why would they do that you?'
'For fun Jack, they don't look like they need any
excuses.' 'Behave yourself Pete.'
'I'll feel better after a couple of bottles of
Prozac.'
Jack laughed at his dry humour while saying
'Pete if you're that worried I'll go myself.'
'I'll be alright Jack.'
'Are you sure?'
'Yeah! I think'
Two days later and Pete was being pushed into
the back of a car at Belfast's city airport and
driven away by three Irishmen, just over an
hour later they pulled into the drive of Sean's

house. It was the first time that Pete had been there and he was genuinely terrified, and at one stage when an army helicopter hovered overhead Pete was visibly shaken. Pete had quite a long chat with Sean before Sean's men took him back to the airport in time to catch the evening flight into Liverpool. Pete headed to Jack's house and explained the situation to him. Jack was bewildered. Three days later, Jack booked into the Britannia hotel in Manchester where he was to meet Sean. Jack was sat at a table in the restaurant when Sean and three other large men walked in; they exchanged pleasantries then sat down and ordered their meals. After they had all finished eating the three men went to the bar while Jack and Sean went to Jack's room to have a private chat. Sean told Jack that they were interested in all the items that Pete had told them about, but the Torah was of the most interest as they had someone interested in it.

'They want twenty million dollars for it.' Jack stressed.

'They'll come down, Sean said, negotiate with them.'

'I'll do what I can.'

'They'll come down quite a bit on that price.' Sean said confidently. 'I hope that you're right.'

With business out of the way the two men returned to the bar to meet up with the three

other men, they later moved on to a couple of the many disco's that were within the hotel complex. Jack was falling asleep on his feet as he entered his hotel room just before three o'clock; he fell asleep fully dressed on top of the bed waking only a few hours later when a chambermaid entered his room to clean it not knowing that Jack was there, on realising that he was there she soon made a swift exit, but by then the short disturbance had woken Jack to the mornings light and there would be no going back to sleep for him. A few days later he was back at the Turks house asking him for some evidence that he actually had these treasures especially evidence that he had the Torah 'It will take time.' The Turk said.
'How much time, Jack demanded, a couple of hours.'
'The Turk laughed, 'A couple of hours…the stuff is not even in this country.'
'Not in this country, Jack growled, what the fuck do you mean?'
'Let me explain to you my friend there are governments and their agents desperately trying to get their hands on these treasures especially the Torah and let me tell you that most of these people will be taking no prisoners, so the last thing that I'll be doing is keeping any of it near to me.'
'That's understandable, but where the fuck is it?'

'If you and your people are definitely interested I'll arrange a meeting for you with the right people.'
'I thought you were the right person.'
'Over here I am, but there are bigger people than me involved in this.'
'Well I suppose you'll have to set up a meeting.'
'When for?'
'As soon as possible, where will it be?'
'Probably in Istanbul.'
'Istanbul.' Jack shrieked.
'Where else?'
'Somewhere local might be handy.' Jack stated.
'Not if you want to see some evidence that we've got these treasures.'
'Istanbul it will have to be then.' Jack moaned.
The two men parted company and as Jack drove homeward he thought to himself that he was not happy having to explain to the Irish firm this latest turn of events. Jack rang Sean's mobile phone and found that Sean was still in England; they arranged to meet the following day at Henry's bar in Manchester. Sean didn't seem a little bit concerned about the news that Jack had brought him he said that he'd send someone to the meeting in Istanbul, but he insisted that Jack should be there to oversee the meeting himself and not just send one of his men to deal with it, although uncomfortable with the situation Jack agreed to go to Istanbul and deal with the situation. It was more than four weeks later following numerous

meetings with people from both sides of the deal that Jack finally arrived at The Hilton Hotel in Istanbul. Jack who was tired due to the previous nights lack of sleep plus the boring flight and on top of that he was also sweaty from the stuffy journey from the airport to the hotel in the soaring heat and in a taxi that was made before the invention of air conditioning. Jack stripped off his clothes and threw them onto the large bed; he stood in the shower for quite some time, enjoying the clean fresh water running over his naked body, he felt refreshed. Jack had only just left the shower and wrapped himself in towels when the phone rang, it was the man at the reception desk telling Jack that there was someone downstairs who would like to meet him, and that they would wait for him in the bar. Jack rubbed the towels furiously against his body to rid himself of any wetness the warm air blown onto his body by the ceiling fan swirling above him helped to dry him quickly; Jack was soon dressed in an open neck shirt and a pair of lightweight trousers, he entered the air conditioned saloon and sat at the bar, it was not long before he was approached by a short squat balding man with an Irish accent.
'You must be Jack?' the man said.
'And you're?' said Jack waiting for an answer to his unfinished question. 'I'm Pat.' said the chirpy little man, 'I'm a friend of Sean's.' 'That's a coincidence, so am I' said Jack grinning.
'Small world.' said the now smiling man.

The two men sat at a table talking about the ills of the world and many other topics they debated, laughed and joked but both deliberately avoided discussing the job in hand, before parting company they agreed to meet up the next day when Sean's antique expert would be there. Jack went back to his room and lay on top of his bed being fanned by the huge blades spinning above him he soon drifted into a deep sleep. The next day Jack and Pat were sat together in the bar when they were approached by the most beautiful of women, Jack thought her to be in her mid thirties a redhead with a striking figure and wonderfully large breasts that she obviously used to there full advantage.
Pat stood up and said, 'This is Maria.'
Jack standing up and taking her hand said, 'It's nice to meet you.'
'I'm a friend of Sean's.' she said in a broad Irish accent.
'Isn't everybody?' Jack replied. They all looked at each other and laughed.
'I suppose you're right.' Maria answered.
'Time for business, Pat said, when can we have a look at the prize?'
'I don't know, now that you're both here I can ring this number that I've been given.' 'Give it a ring then.' Pat demanded.
'Is it safe to ring from here?' Jack asked.
'I don't know, said Pat, but the choices are going to be limited over here.'

'I suppose so, said Jack adding, we'll soon find out if they're not.' Jack went to use the public telephone in the foyer of the hotel; on his return he explained to the other two that someone would be coming to the hotel to see them later that day. The three of them decided to stay in the air conditioned bar and wait for the arrival of the mystery man; It was some two hours before the man arrived they had all eaten a light meal and consumed several beverages while they had been waiting for him to make an appearance. The man from the reception desk had sent a young girl with him to show him where they were sat in the saloon bar area. The young girl pointed out to him where they were sat, he gave her a tip and she turned and walked away. The dark skinned man dressed in robes of middle eastern nature approached their table and in broken English asked if one of them was Jack. Jack nodded and said who he was, the man introduced himself has Abi and said that he had been sent to speak to Jack and to bring Jack and his friends to the town of Cizre the look on the two Irish faces was enough to tell Jack that there was something wrong. Jack quizzed the man as to why they would have to travel to Cizre and Abi's reply was that this is where they would be shown the Torah and anything else that they wished to see. The man now known as Abi left their company promising to return the next day

to collect them and take them all to Cizre to see the treasures. As soon as Abi was out of earshot heading for the door Pat said, 'He's got to be fuckin joking.' 'About what.' Jack asked. 'If he thinks I'm going anywhere with him.'
'Or me,' Maria butted in.
'Why, what's the matter?'
'Do you know anything about Cizre?'
'No.'
'I thought not, it's fuckin bandit country, the law of the gun like the wild west used to be only these fuckin lot have got Uzi's and Kalashnikovs, and there ain't no sheriff to bail you out if you get into trouble.'
'So it could be a little dangerous eh?'
'A little dangerous.' Pat blurted out.
The three of them sat around for a while trying to find a solution to what tomorrow would become a problem. They decided that their options were limited to firstly throwing their hand in and returning home, secondly they could all go to Cizre and if it went wrong and they all got killed there would be no one left to tell the story, or thirdly which they all agreed would be the best plan was that just one of them would go with Abi to Cizre, and then he or she would check out the goods and report back to the others in Istanbul before they made the next move. Pat declared that he was neither an adventurer nor of any use with the examination of antiques. Maria for her part although

declaring to be somewhat of an antique expert was not the least bit interested in going off into the unknown with Abi and his friends. 'So I'm volunteered for the fuckin job am I?' Jack snapped angrily. 'Well there is no one else.' said Maria.
'It still doesn't cheer me up, said Jack, and what do I know about antiques?'
'I'll explain what I need you to do.' said Maria. She went on to explain to Jack that he would need to take a couple of cameras with him to photograph the Torah and whatever other items that they turned- up with. It was a long uncomfortable journey to Cizre by road the battered old minibus the six men travelled in took them three and a half days to get there passing Mount Arrat in the distance and then closely passing the heavily guarded Syrian border on their way, there were soldiers dug in behind stacks of sandbags, there were barbed wire fences with skull and cross bones signs to warn of landmines and Syrian troop carriers were a common sight on the other side of the wire fences. The town of Cizre itself was made up of little white buildings huddled together some were little communes with courtyards there were people on every corner staring at the minibus as it passed by and when Jack finally alighted the vehicle everyone in the whole street came to stare at him it was a paranoid schizophrenics worst nightmare. Jack was taken into a house with the interpreter that had been

brought with them from Istanbul there were already several men inside the house and many more armed with rifles left on guard outside. The interpreter introduced Jack to the men, they in turn put their arms around him in a welcoming manner, one of them who spoke some English said 'You IRA: I am PKK you are my brother,' Jack tried to explain to them that he was not in the IRA but either they did not understand or they didn't want to. He thought it might be best if he let them believe that he was IRA he also thought that it might give him an extra chance of surviving for another day if they believed that he was not acting alone. Jack followed the men into a courtyard where they opened a wooden box which had two protruding handles at each end similar he thought to those of a rolling pin, the box folded open into two halves, showing that the handles were attached to a huge scroll, the men unrolled the scroll along the courtyard it was about thirty metres long and looked to be made of some form of animal skin cut into squares about eighteen inches high by two feet wide and each square sewn to the next to make the complete scroll, upon the scroll was an unusual writing very neat and tidy Jack thought it to be written in old Hebrew but he wasn't sure. Jack opened the small bag that he had brought with him and put his hand inside it, he turned around quickly as he heard the sound of many guns click to the ready, he stopped and stared at the many guns that were pointing in his direction, he slowly took his empty hand from the bag, at that time one of the tribesmen came over and in one swift motion of picking the bag from the ground he scattered the contents onto the floor of the courtyard. There were only rulers, papers, a video camera, and a normal instamatic; Maria had given this equipment to Jack so that he could gather the proof that she needed to prove the existence of the Torah. Jack explained through the interpreter what he needed to do but they would not let him near the cameras, they seemed to be afraid that he would film or photograph them even though most of the tribesmen were covered from head to toe in their tribal wear, only part of their faces or eyes were seen. The tribesmen's leader decided that they would do the job for him so Jack had to explain what he wanted them to do, he told them that they had to video the whole thing, they had to lay the rulers down alongside the Torah and photograph it clearly to show the measurements, the men did what Jack told them to the letter but when it was over they put the equipment back into Jack's bag but wouldn't give him his bag back, Jack was taken back to the minibus where all the men who came with him boarded the vehicle then they set about the long arduous journey back to Istanbul. On his return to the Hilton hotel Jack showered then went to bed, he never resurfaced for almost thirty-six hours. He was eventually aroused from his sleep by the tapping on his door; Jack crawled from his

comfortable bed and opened the door. 'Thank God for that.' Maria blurted out.
'For what?' Jack quizzed.
'That you're still alive, we were getting worried.'
'we?'
'Yes me and Pat.'
'Right, right,' Jack said still trying to wake himself up.
'Did you see it?'
'See it?' Jack declared.
'Yes, yes, did you see the Torah? Did you film and photograph it all.'
'Well someone did, they wouldn't let me do it myself.'
'Why not?'
'I'll explain it to you one day.'
'Okay I'll look forward to it, but for now show me the video.' 'Er, slight problem there.'
'What problem?
'I haven't got it.'
'You haven't got it, ... Where is it?'
'I don't know.'
'What do you mean?'
'I mean, they took the bag with the cameras in and didn't return it, so at this moment in time I've not got a clue where it is.'
'What did the interpreter say?'
'He doesn't know either.'
'That's great, just great.' She moaned.
Jack got dressed and then the two of them went

to look for Pat and finding him in the bar, they explained the situation to Pat and after thinking about it for a few minutes he said, 'They'll be in touch.'

'What makes you think that?' asked Maria. 'Because they've got something that they want to sell, it's too hot to handle for most people, and they think that we can do something with it, they'll be in touch.' 'I hope that you're right.' Mumbled Maria.

'So do I' said Jack, hoping that he hadn't been through all that terror and trouble for nothing. The next day when Jack was making his way to the bar to meet up with Maria and Pat the man on the reception desk called him over, Jack walked over to him and the man handed Jack a package addressed to him, Jack took it and walked through to the bar area where he met Maria and Pat they sat at a table where Jack unwrapped the package to find his bag with all the equipment inside, Maria snatched up the video camera after checking that there was a tape in it and by looking into the viewfinder as she played back the tape she was able to view the Torah. She moaned with delight and at times shrieked with excitement as she viewed the mysterious treasures. 'It's all wonderful.' She declared. 'Is that Torah the genuine article?' Jack wanted to know. 'I'd stake my life on it.' Maria volunteered.

'It may be an accepted bet.' Said Pat taking the

camera from her.
'And all the other stuff the paintings, the gold coins they all look genuine too.' 'Paintings, gold coins,' Jack said has he snatched the camera from Pat,
'I didn't see any of that, this PKK mob must have filmed it after I'd left, the crafty bastards.' 'Maybe it was somewhere else Jack, and they didn't want you to see exactly where, and it saved them carting stuff about all over the show, they just took advantage of the camera, quite clever really.' Mused Pat.
'I suppose it was really.' Said Jack, taking the camera from his eye and staring at Maria who in turn was beaming like a Cheshire cat.
'Something amusing you Maria?' Jack asked.
'I can't believe what we're looking at.' She beamed.
'I don't want to believe what we're looking at if we get caught.' Jack added.
'Nor Me.' Added Pat.
'What happens next?' Maria asked the two men.
'For you, Jack said, you need to report back to Sean and let him know your findings.'
Will do,' she said as she stood up.
'Where are you going?' Jack asked.
'To the phone to ring Sean.' She replied.
'No,' snapped Jack, you must tell him in person, don't use the phones here.'
'We'll organise some flights tomorrow.' said

the nodding Pat.

Jack was woken early the next morning by someone knocking on his door, when he opened it, he found the interpreter that had travelled with him to Cizre, Jack let him into the room the man had a large carpet bag with him, he opened it and took from it one of the oblong pieces from the Torah. Jack went to Maria's room and woke her from her slumber then practically dragging her with some haste along the hallway to his room he showed her the animal skin which he told her was a part of the Torah. She recognised it straight away, she was ecstatic, she tried to quiz the interpreter several times about the Torah and the other treasures but he remained silent, although she was fully sure that what she had before her was the genuine article she went off to get some equipment from her room, by the time she had returned to Jack's room the interpreter had long gone, saying very little has he packed the Torah into his bag, throwing the strap over his shoulder and disappearing just as mysteriously has he had arrived. 'Where is he?' she screamed on her return carrying two boxes of equipment.
'Gone.' Jack said casually.
'Gone, what do you mean gone, why didn't you stop him.'
'Yeah,' laughed Jack, 'He's probably got half a dozen men outside somewhere tooled up to the bollox, with Kalashnikovs and the like, and you

want me to grab hold of him in some sort of kamikaze headlock, you can think again sister.' Maria Just shrieked out loud, made some comment about men that Jack just couldn't decipher and turning on her heels she stormed off back to her room. Jack went down to the bar later where he met Pat, there was no sign of the angry Maria. Pat told Jack that he'd sorted out flights to Heathrow for the following evening and that Jack would have to make his own arrangements from there. Jack explained to Pat about the interpreter coming and going in a mysterious manner and that Maria had thrown her dummy out of the pram and stormed off. Pat finished his drink and went to find Maria to try to calm her down; he would use the news about the flights as an excuse for seeking her out. The next day Jack, Pat, and Maria boarded a flight for London Heathrow England, where upon arrival Pat and Maria would set off for Ireland while Jack would head north westward to either Manchester or Liverpool airport, from whichever he could get a flight to the soonest.

Chapter five

By the time Jack clambered out of the taxi it was just gone two in the morning, he could see that his house was in darkness as he approached the front door. He sneaked in quietly so has not to disturb Sandra, he had hardly taken a step into the room when all hell broke loose, as the security alarm kicked into action, startling Jack and causing Sandra to jump out of bed in a panic and lock the bedroom door. Jack spent a few minutes fumbling around before he finally punched in the right sequence of numbers and silenced the menacing racket, before climbing the stairway to his bedroom, on finding the door locked he tapped gently on the door, only to be answered by Sandra demanding who it was, on hearing Jack's voice she quickly opened the door and flew into his arms, where they held on to each other for quite some time. The next day having rested and now feeling somewhat refreshed Jack drove to Pete's house where Jack explained all the goings on to Pete by the time Jack had finished talking, Pete was mortified;
'We're getting into something here that's a bit to heavy for us Jack.'
'If it comes off it's an earner Pete, we never know where it will lead!'

'It might lead to us going missing Jack, it's like living out a fucking spy movie.'
'Yeah, and without the girl.' Jack smiled.
'What girl?' Pete asked.
'You know, the Bond girl, he always gets the girl.'
'Oh right, I wondered what the fuck you were on about then.'
'We're wandering off on a bit of a tangent.'
'You can say that again, and before you do, don't bother it's not funny.'
'Not to you?'
'No, anyway I've got a story for you.'
'What about?'
'Well do you remember me telling you about Phil Pearce from that garage and scrap yard on Pontefract Road, Broomhill in Barnsley.'
'Yeah, he got set up by the odd-lot and nicked.'
'Well Jack the plot thickens, Phil only tried to do a deal with the odd-lot and wangle himself out of the charges by turning grass and by pulling his mate into the conspiracy by making up some bollocks that it was nothing to do with him and it was his mate who had set the deal up.'
'Well I thought he'd been caught bang to rights.'
'He was.'
'Well there's no benefit in him grassing anyone

else up then is there?'
'No, absolutely none, but that's what he's done, maybe he was frightened of going to jail on his own.'
'The dirty grassing shithouse.'
'Well he always was suspect Jack, he looks like a grass.'
'That's coz he his, …..time has proved that to be right.'
'He looks like a fucking nonce too.'
'Well that wouldn't surprise me either with that pompous twat.'
'Yeah he probably hangs around kiddies playgrounds with his bag of sweeties.'
'Yeah him and his mates from the fuckin odd-lot.'
'That fuckin odd-lot, now most of them do look like fuckin paedo's, the dirty orrible bastards.'
'Have they been weighed off yet?'
'Who?'
Pearce and the guy that he grassed up.'
Yeah, Pearce got nicked with the conspiracy to import nine hundred grams of amphetamine charge, plus ten more kilos of amphetamine that they found in his house and a kilo of pot and on top of that they found two stolen motorcycles in his garage; he got three and a half years.
'And what happened to the guy who he grassed up?'
'Well he only got done on the first charge of conspiracy to import the 900 grams of

amphetamine.'
'What did he get for that?'
'Five years.'
'Five fuckin years.' Jack shouted, 'how do they work that one out.'
'Well as you can see that alone tells a story.'
'Oh, it tells a fuckin story alright.'
'Yeah Jack, it tells a story of a fuckin stitch up.'
'Don't we know it?'
'British fuckin Justice eh!'
'Now there's an oxymoron.'
'An oxywhaton! What's one of them?'
'It's when two words are used in a sentence and one of the words cancels the other one out.'
'I don't follow that?'
'Simple really, you can't have British and Justice in the same fucking sentence because in the police state called Britain there's no such thing has Justice the whole fuckin system is corrupt from top to bottom.'
'We all know that Jack, but it will never change.'
'You're right mate one rule for them and one rule for us, anyway we keep wandering off on these tangents lets get back to business, we've got things to do, the odd shilling to be earned so time to crack on.' Jack told Pete that he had finally got all the right people in the right places to do the cig deals he was only waiting for Seamus' friends in Gibraltar to confirm that they

were ready and the plan would go into action, he explained that he was going to run two different deals at the same time, one with Roger and one with Angel that way if one fell over he still had a chance with the other. Pete thought that it was a good plan and he was hopeful that he could earn some decent money which in turn might cheer up his beloved wife Jane. They had to wait another four weeks before the first wagon load of cigarettes arrived at Angels warehouse and because Angel had his own buyers, Jack and Pete could keep well away from any of the action that is until the next day when Roger's load arrived although Roger had storage capabilities he had no buyers and that's where Jack and Pete came in, Jack had already pre-warned Mohammed that there was a container of °; due that day, but Jack delayed the delivery for a couple of days just to make sure that the truck was in the clear before Pete went to move it to Mohammed's warehouse two days later all the cigs were gone and Jack and Pete took another two days to count the money after most of the overheads were paid there was a substantial profit 'We're in the money.' Pete shouted with joy. The smile disappearing from his face when Jack said seriously 'Well I am.'
'What do ya mean Jack?' Pete said choking on his words.
'Fuckinell Pete, I'm only joking, don't look so fuckin miserable.'

'It's no fuckin wonder that someone is trying to kill you ……you're a fuckin wind up bastard, …if you do that to me one more time, I'll kill you meself.'
'That's a bit anti-social Pete.'
'Is that all you've got to say?'
'That, and when we've buried some of this dosh out of the way, we'll go and spread some of our new found wealth at the steakhouse I'm starving, and I need a breather after doing all this money counting.'
'Me too.'
'I'm going to nip home for a shower and to let Sandra know that I'll be going for a scran with you later.'
'Yeah, I could do with a shower meself, what time should I meet you?'
The two chatted about nonsense has they ate their meals Jack having his normal orange juice and Pete having a couple of beers, Jack had told him not to drink any more than that `loose lips sink ships' Jack had whispered to him, they devoured their main course and decided that while it was a special occasion that they would indulge in a dessert; they were like kids in a sweet shop when the large knickerbockerglory ice creams arrived at their table together with a couple of elongated thin spoons that would help them to get to the bottom of the long glass container, if they did actually get that far, Pete had only just got past the whipped cream

topping and he was already starting to look a little bit green, Jack didn't fair much better when he pushed the giant glass tumbler towards the centre of the table saying `I think our eyes are bigger than our bellies mate' the ill looking Pete just nodded. Pete disappeared to the loo while Jack finished his coffee and paid the bill. `Happy days are here again' Jack thought smiling to himself. The two men left the restaurant and walked slowly towards their vehicles as they reached the middle of the road a car that was slowly passing by suddenly accelerated towards them, on hearing the revving engine the two men dove towards other parked vehicles to use them as a shield against the fast approaching missile, Jack somehow managed to get clear but Pete got clipped by the accelerating vehicle sending him head first over the bonnet of a parked car landing rather shaken on the pavement Pete lay there dazed as Jack ran over to where he lay. 'You okay?' Jack shouted.

'Yeah, I'll survive, but it's ruined the good day that I was having.'

'And mine too.' Jack said solemnly. Jack took hold of Pete's hand and helped to pull him to his feet. 'Are you hurt Pete?'

'Just a bit of a bang on my leg, ..what the fuck was all that about' 'I'm not sure Pete, maybe it was someone pissed up falling asleep at the wheel.'

'No, that was to close for comfort, someone aimed that car at us deliberately.'
'You can't be sure?'
'Well he hasn't fuckin stopped to apologise.'
'No, you're right there, and he's managed to hit a few of these cars, before he fucked off.' Just has Jack had finished talking there was a screech of tyres alongside him and Pete, the car door was thrown open and a uniformed policeman got out and asked them what was going on has the police had received a phone call from the restaurant saying that someone had been run over. 'We never saw anything, did we Pete?' 'No, not a thing.'
'Well how come you're both wet and covered in bits of stone chippings off the road.' asked the policeman.
'We fell over.' Jack answered.
The policeman told them to stay where they were while he went to the restaurant to speak to whoever had called the police, no sooner had he entered the restaurant doorway than Jack said to Pete that he'd meet him the next day and they both jumped into their own cars and slipped away into the night leaving the unsuspecting policeman with another mystery to think about.

Chapter six

The morning after the night before and Jack was beginning to feel the bumps and bruises on his ageing body after his sudden burst of athleticism the previous night. Jack's mobile phone rang in the distance, and Jack rubbed his sore back as he hobbled away to find the noisy object. It was Angel wanting to have a meeting later in the day; Jack agreed to meet him and then having disconnected his call to Angel he rang Pete to invite him to the little get-together, Pete complained about his swollen leg but still agreed to be at the meeting. When Jack and Pete who had met on the car park walked into the pub together they spotted Angel straight away. He saw them enter and was having little fits of laughter as the two injured men hobbled towards his table. 'What the fuck happened to you two?' said the beaming laughing man. 'You don't want to know.' Jack replied.
'But I do.' Laughed the beaming man.
'Well we're not telling.' Said the smirking Pete.
'Come on then chaps take a seat, that's if you can manage it on your own.'
'You don't worry about us sitting down, you just worry about whether you can get back up again ya fat bastard.' Jack grinned.

'Now, now chaps no need to get personal, I'm only having a laugh.'
'So are we.' Jack answered. The three men sat down to chat whereupon Angel volunteered that the people who he had sold the cigs to were now screaming at him as to when he could supply some more and he in turn wanted to know the same from Jack. Jack told Angel that he could not give him an answer until he had spoken to some of the other people that were involved; he did however believe that there would be more work shortly but he didn't know exactly when that would be. Jack promised that he would ring Angel as soon as he had more information. A few minutes later Jack and Pete hobbled towards the door not looking back to see that the grinning man was watching them as they made their exit. Jack and Pete parted company on the car park and both men went home; Jack on entering his house found the mobile that he'd left behind ringing away, as he picked it up in the hallway he could see that there had been several missed calls, 'Hello' Jack shouted into the phone.
'Is that you Jack?'
'Yes, who's that?'
'It's Sean, I've been trying to get hold of you for ages.'
'Have you, why?'
'I'm coming over to England the day after tomorrow, and I'd like to have a meet, if that's alright with you?'

'It's alright with me.' Jack replied.
The two men discussed where they would meet and then on ending their conversation there was a click and the phones were silenced. Jack sat down in his armchair with a hot cup of tea in his hand, and mulled over the past few weeks events from almost being at a standstill, just dawdling along doing the same old thing week after week, to getting involved with the IRA and the Kurdish PKK seeing the mysterious Torah plus all the other treasures that they'd videoed for his perusal, then successfully acquiring and quickly selling a couple of container loads of cigarettes all that plus a couple more attempts on his life by a mysterious assailant or assailants, it all seemed surreal to Jack it was like watching a weird dream unfold before him; to Jack's mind it had all happened in the blink of an eye, everything had moved very quickly and luckily enough for him he was still alive and except for a few bumps and bruises he was still in one piece and financially he was way out in front of the game. There's always a downside thought Jack and he wondered what it would be. He sometimes wondered when his nine lives were going to run out, he wasn't quite sure how many he'd used up, but he thought it might be more than nine already, a million thoughts and memories ran through his mind and as he wandered deeper into thought he drifted to sleep on his armchair, the now empty tea cup lying still in his lap. Jack woke in the early hours,

uncomfortable and stiff from his awkward sleeping position, he struggled to his feet and with one hand pressing onto his back, he clambered the stairs to the bedroom whereupon he slipped into his warm comfortable bed next to his beloved Sandra, it was not long before Jack was fast asleep again. It was late morning when Jack awoke again, Sandra had already vanished from their bed, and Jack had considered lying cocooned in his warm duvet for a while longer but the smell of freshly made bread that had found its way from the kitchen to his bedroom was now tantalising his taste buds and forcing him to exit the bedroom in search of nourishment. As Jack entered the kitchen another smell, the smell of cooking bacon entered his nasal passageway causing him to lick his lips in anticipation has his now rumbling belly began to expect the arrival of food.

'So you're up then.' Sandra smiled.

'Just about, he said, and I'm starving.'

'I was coming to get you in a minute, when I'd done your breakfast.'

'I could smell the bread.'

'I thought you might.' She grinned.

Jack sat down to his breakfast feast and slowly but surely devoured the whole meal and has his brain flicked from one thought to another trying to put his near future plans into some form of order. He would not be meeting Sean until the following day, so if there
was anything that needed to be arranged quickly it

would have to be done in whatever time was left of this day for he knew that he would not be available the next day, on the other hand it was possible that he may not be available for many more days coming depending on the outcome of the meeting with Sean. The day passed uneventfully has no one rang Jack, and he was happy to pass the day away quietly with Sandra while the children were at school. The meeting with Sean in Manchester the following day was a bit of a blur with two of Sean's men arriving first then when Sean turned up he only whispered a few words to Jack before leaving again. Jack headed for home again thinking about what Sean had said to him as he drove along the motorway; he was also thinking that he needed to speak to the Turk as soon as possible. Jack stopped in a lay-by after he left the motorway to use the public phone box; he rang Pete and told him that he needed him to set up a meeting with the Turk for as soon as possible, Pete said that he'd get on to it straight away, Jack said that he'd see him later and at that the call ended. Before going home Jack called to see Mohammed to ask him how the cigarette business was doing, and according to Mohammed it was the best thing since sliced bread he was another one who was desperate for another delivery. After leaving Mohammed's warehouse Jack called at another public telephone box to ring Seamus in Spain to find out when the Gibraltan people would be able to organise more papers to be signed, Seamus told him that he'd find out and get back to him, he also wanted to know when his cut of the deal would be forthcoming, Jack told him that everything was in hand and he would be in touch with him soon. Pete set up a meeting with the Turk and Jack went down to meet him, it was only a brief meeting; Jack offered the Turk ten million dollars for the Torah which was only half of the original price that the Turk had asked for, the Turk said that he'd have to discuss it with his people and he would be back in touch when he had an answer. Jack stopped off at a Motorway service station and used a public telephone to ring Sean, he told Sean that he'd made an offer and that he would get back to him as soon as he had an answer. Seamus had left a text message on Jack's phone for Jack to get in touch with him, which he did as soon as he'd read the message. 'What's happening Seamus?'

'Is that you Jack?'

'Sure is, I've just got your message.'

'Good, I couldn't get hold of you, do you ever take that phone with you?'

'Sometimes.' Jack laughed.

'Right, the Gibraltan mob can only slip one of those jobs in every few months otherwise it will be noticed and then the whole job will be fucked, best to have a bit every now and then, than to try and rush the job and finish up with nothing at all.' 'I make you right mate.'

'I'll let you know when they're ready to go again.'

Seamus said thoughtfully.
'Whenever you're ready mate, give us a shout.'
'I will pal, you just don't forget to send my dosh.'
'As though?' Jack laughed.
'I'll be hearing from you then.'
'Course you will.'
'Make it soon I'm skint.'
'Down to your last ten million then.'
'I've not got ten million pence.'
'Hmmmm, I'll get back to you soon.'
'Okay.'
There was a click and the phones were silent once more.
Jack went to see Angel to give him the bad news; he was hoping that this cig deal was going to be a bit more regular than every few months but alas as it was not to be they agreed that they would have to look at other methods of earning the odd shilling.
'If anything comes up I'll give you a shout.' Jack called to Angel as he got into his car.
'Cheers' Angel shouted back as Jack's car engine roared into action. On his way home Jack stopped off at a public telephone box to pass on the same news to Roger and Mohammed. Several days later Pete called to arrange a meeting with Jack in the Mucky Duck. 'What's happening Pete?' said the chirpy Jack as he sat down next to Pete.
'Just a message from the Turk, he say's that

they won't take less than eleven.'
'I think that will be acceptable, tell them to get it sorted and I'll get the other side of the deal sorted out.'
'No problem Jack, ... do you know what you're getting involved in here?'
'No, but I think it's easier to go forward than to try to pull out now, we would upset a lot of people.'
'I think that we've already upset someone.
'Who?'
'Whoever's taking pot shots at us.'
'They're enough, without upsetting anyone else Pete.'
'Suppose you're right, I'll ring the Turk tomorrow.'
'Yeah, there's no rush, no-ones going anywhere, not on this deal anyway.'
'Anything else happening?'
'Only the usual.'
'That's enough for me, I need a rest, and a permanent one from this puff business it's not worth a dinar.'
'What are we making?'
'Peanuts Jack, some weeks we're hardly breaking even, by the time we take our overheads into consideration it's touch and go whether we win or lose.'
'Wrap it up Pete, we're not working and risking our necks on that kind of a profit margin, bollocks to it, we've made a few quid off the cigs so that will tide us over for a while, we're bound to come up with

something else.'
'Are you sure?'
'Positive, lets have an adventure, try new pastures before we get to old.'
'Aye, if we get old, with all these murderous attempts on you which there's a possibility of and I might get caught up in another one.'
'It keeps you on your toes.'
'On my toes, I'm a nervous fuckin wreck.' Pete shrieked. 'What are you worried about?'
'Well in case its slipped your mind some lunatic in a doctor's coat tried to kill us when you were in hospital, then another maniac tried to shoot at us at the Highwayman, then some other bastard tried to run us over outside the restaurant and then there's all the other attempts on you when I wasn't there, and you want to know what I'm worried about.' 'Nothing serious then Pete.' Jack said trying to make light of the situation.
'Its not funny Jack.' Said the extremely serious Pete.
'Okay Pete, wrap up any business that's ongoing then you can naff off on holiday for a while, chill out with your Mrs.'
'I'll have some of that.' Pete said as he got up to leave the Mucky Duck.
'You off then Pete.'
'Yeah I'm going home to pack.' Pete laughed.
'Can't blame you mate.' Jack smiled.
The two men left together laughing as they stepped out of the pub onto the car park, Pete

walked towards Sandra's car with Jack, he was excited at the thought of having a break from the business and looking forward to spending some quality time alone with Jane. Just as the two men neared Sandra's car a man in a Balaclava appeared from behind another vehicle next to Sandra's, he jumped out of the darkness pointing a sawn off shotgun at the two men as he ran towards them, the gun clicked but nothing happened, Jack grabbed Pete's arm and swinging him around quickly he catapulted Pete into the masked man, and as the man stumbled backwards Jack was on him like a ton of bricks, he held the struggling man in some sort of headlock for a few minutes until the man struggled no more. Jack looked up to where Pete was standing, 'What have you picked that up for?'

'Uh, I don't know.' said the dazed Pete holding the shotgun. Jack dragged the masked man between two cars so that no one else would see him if they were to enter the dark car park, Jack ripped the mask from the man's head, 'Do you know him Pete?' Pete looked over Jacks shoulder and gasped, 'He's black.'

'Oh very observant Pete, but do you fuckin know him?'

'No, ...I don't think so.'

'Keep watch while I check his pockets.' Jack checked the mans pockets and found only a couple more rounds of ammunition.

'Hurry up Jack before someone comes or he wakes up.' 'He won't be waking up Pete, he's gone.'
'Gone,' Pete said choking on the word,
'What do you mean he's gone, gone where?'
'Pete go and get your car and bring it over here, park it in that other bay, back it in and leave a bit of room at the back.'
'I don't believe this Jack, what's up with your car?' said the now panicking Pete.
'Sandra's car Pete, look at the fucking size of him, I'd have to put him on the fuckin roof rack, and that Pete might attract some attention.'
'Right, alright.' Just has Pete spoke the headlights from an approaching car lit up the car park, the two men stood together pretending to be chatting while blocking the view of the now lifeless man from anyone who happened to pass by. The police car stopped alongside the two men, the window was wound down. 'Good evening chaps,' the constable shouted to them. Jack replied while Pete just stood staring at the policeman. 'You've not seen any strange things going on around here, have you?'
'Such as what?' Jack asked, he could see that Pete was now visibly shaking; Jack was hoping that the constable wouldn't notice. 'There's been a lot of cars broken into just lately around here, I'm just keeping my eye out for anything suspicious.' 'Well as you can see, there's nothing happening tonight.' Jack suggested.

'Well if it does I'll have em, nothing gets past me,' the policeman bragged as he wound his window up.' Jack waved to him as he drove away across the car park. 'I think that I've just pissed myself,' Pete said, 'lets get out of here.' 'Oh yeah, and that copper will have forgotten about us two later when someone finds a body here, go and get your fuckin car.' Pete could not contain himself he was shaking like a leaf as he backed the car into the space where Jack had told him to park, he left the front of the car protruding a little so that there would be room at the back to move about, Pete opened the boot then went the few yards to where Jack was standing and helped him to drag the body along the ground to the back of Pete's car, the two men ever aware that someone may appear out of the blue or even the possibility that the constable may return were foremost in their minds as they struggled to lift the limp heavy body into the boot of Pete's car, once the body was tucked in the boot and out of sight Pete threw the shotgun in alongside it and slammed the boot lid shut. 'Leaving your fingerprints on that boot lid eh Pete?'
'Not a fucking chance.' Said Pete as he frantically rubbed the boot lid with his coat sleeve.
'Well thank fuck that's over.' Jack said.
'What do you mean over Jack, there's a fuckin body of a hitman, a fuckin black

hitman at that in my car and I'm not taking him home.' Pete loudly whispered nervously.
'We're not taking him any where.'
'What do you mean?'
'I mean, back the car up a bit more so it's level with the others, then put one of your ignition keys on the back wheel and leave the door unlocked.' M m m m ,
'Someone might nick my radio.'
'You're worried about a fuckin radio?'
'Just messin Jack.'
'You'd better be, right let's get back into the pub.'
'You're going in there and leaving him here.'
'Well he's not fucking going anywhere is he?'
'Suppose not Jack.' Pete answered as he followed Jack back into the pub.' Pete went to the bar and ordered some drinks while Jack went to the phone.' 'Hello B.T. I've got a job for you.'
'Good because I definitely need some spondooleys.'
'You know the coup.'
'As long as it's not digging more fuckin holes.'
'Well as it happens.'
'Not again.'
'No, don't worry its not so difficult this time, you won't be looking for a needle in a haystack.'
'Thank fuck for that.' Jack explained in coded words where the vehicle was and where he

could find the key; he also explained that there was some rubbish in the boot that needed getting rid of. B.T. understood the situation and no sooner had he put the phone down, than he threw on his coat and set off on his way. It was over two hours later just as Jack and Pete were finishing a meal when Jack's mobile rang to let him know that the skip was empty of the rubbish. 'It's time for us to go Pete.' Jack said as he pushed the plate towards the centre of the table. 'Okay.' Said the now calmer Pete. The two men once again left the pub and stepped onto the car park this time having a good look around for any would be assassins, they walked across the car park when Pete shouted aloud, 'My fuckin cars gone, someone's nicked me car.'
'Oh dear,' said Jack, 'We'll have to report it to the police.'
'The police.' Pete said slowly.
The two men returned to the pub and Pete used the public telephone box to ring the police and report his vehicle stolen, twenty minutes later the constable who they had seen earlier pulled onto the pub car park. 'It's small world,' he said. 'innit.' said Pete.
The constable took Pete's details from him and said he'd let him know if they found his car. Jack then gave Pete a lift home before going home himself. 'You've been gone a long time.' Sandra said.

'Yeah, something came up.'
'Doesn't it always with you Dunkerley.' Sandra laughed.
The following morning Pete was woken by a loud banging on his door, he jumped from his bed to see two policemen standing there, he knocked on the window to let them know that he had heard them, before wandering downstairs to answer the door, only one of the policemen spoke, he said that he was there to let him know that his stolen car had been found burnt out twenty odd miles away and that it was up to him to have it removed or the local council would have it moved and then they would bill him for it. Pete took the details from them about where the car could be found but in his own mind he never wanted to see that car again, he genuinely didn't know who had taken it and he didn't want to know either, that was Jack's department. Pete got Jane out of bed and told her to pack. He let Jack know where the burnt out car had been left and Jack said he'd deal with it. Two hours later Pete and Jane got into a taxi and headed for the airport. 'Where are we going Pete?' Jane asked.
'Somewhere nice.' Pete answered, but not even knowing himself until he got to the airport and checked out the last minute flights desk.

Chapter seven

'Hello' Jack said as he answered his mobile phone.
'It's me Jack... B.T.'
'Everything alright?'
'Yeah fine, Iwas just wondering if you were coming to see me .... about the .... er .. job.'
'I'll be up to see you later, I've got nothing else on today.'
'Cheers mate, that'll be great ... any idea what time?'
'I'll give you a ring before I leave.'
'See you later then.'
Jack pressed the button on his phone which terminated the call to B.T. and no sooner had he done that when the phone in his hand burst into life once more. 'Hello'
'Hello Jack.' The accent giving away the identity of the caller.
'Hello Sean.' Jack replied having recognised the voice of the Irishman.
'I'll be over your way tomorrow, any chance of getting together?'
'Same place at seven.' Jack offered.
'Make it eight to allow for error.' Sean laughed.
'Eight it is then.' Jack agreed.

Later that day Jack made an appearance at B.T.'s house where he gave him a brown envelope.
'I think you'll find that what's in there will cover your expenses.'
'Cheers Jack, give me a shout if any more work comes up I need the dosh.'
'Spent your bit from the Scottish then?'
'Drunk it mate, well most of it, surprising how many friends you inherit after a few beers.'
'Well that few quid should stop the brewery from going bust for a while.' Jack said as he pointed at the envelope.
'You might be right.' B.T. grinned.
B.T. walked Jack back to his car; they said their goodbyes and Jack drove off towards the motorway. The following day Jack booked himself into the Britannia hotel in Piccadilly Manchester by the time he'd got washed and changed and walked down to the restaurant it was almost eight o'clock. Jack sat at a table and waited for Sean to arrive, he ordered a coffee while he waited. Jack was just finishing his second coffee when Sean arrived, he apologised for being late, the two men then ordered their meals and while they were waiting for the first course they got down to business.
'Did you negotiate a better deal for the Torah?' Sean asked.
'Yes' Jack smiled.
'And what would that be?' Sean whispered.

'Fifteen million dollars.' said Jack without batting an eyelid.
'We'll take the deal at that; we've got people in America desperate to get their hands on it.'
'Rather them than me.' Jack said thoughtfully.
'One mans food is another mans poison.' Proclaimed the Irishman. 'Suppose it is.' Muttered Jack.

'Have you got any prices for the paintings yet?'
'No, none of the other goodies either.'
'You'll have to go back to Istanbul Jack.'
'Will I fuck.' Jack snapped.

'I need to send a man to look at the rest of the stuff, Pat and Maria will be out there too, but they're too terrified to travel to Gizre.'

'I can't fucking blame them, it's not Disney world ya know.'
'I know its not but there's enough money in this job for every one to come out with a nice little pension.'
'I'll think about it.' Jack said thoughtfully.
'Don't take to long, we need to sort the Torah deal out soon as well.'
'How's that going to work?'
'Easy, you'll bring the Torah to us and we'll give you the fifteen million dollars.'
'Yeah, ... and I'm a fuckin china man, you can well fuck that idea right off, there's not a prayer of that happening.'
'Calm down Jack.'
'I am calm.'

'Hmmm, don't worry we'll sort something out, one way or another.'
'Another sounds good to me.'
'It would do to you Jack, where's your sense of fair play.'
'Fair play, Jack shouted, I think I've done my fair share of running about, living on adrenalin.'
'Maybe your right, I'm sure that we'll work something out.'
A few days later Jack booked into the Hilton hotel in Istanbul, after a quick wash he went down to the bar where he found Pat and Maria, Pat gripped Jack's hand in a show of friendship whereas Maria Leaned forward and kissed Jack on both cheeks, Jack whispered something to her and she blushed, Jack smiled and turned to Pat and has Pat was speaking, another man had now joined them.
'This is Mike.' Pat said introducing Mike to Jack. Jack shook the offered hand. 'Nice to meet you Jack.' Mike said politely in an unmistakable American accent. 'And you.' Jack replied.
The four people sat together at a table in the corner away from prying eyes and ears while they discussed the business that was to be done. It was agreed that Mike would go with Jack to Gizre to look at the stolen treasures. The next day Jack and Mike together with the interpreter Abi and six other tribesmen set off for Gizre. Jack had travelled this long and perilous

journey once before but nothing could prepare him for such a task, Mike however had not travelled so far in such a manner before and he was not feeling to well after the first day, the food was terrible the temperature was boiling and the stench of the sweating tribesmen was making him physically sick, the van had to stop a couple of times to let him get out to throw up and on another occasion he stuck his head out of the window has he puked out on to the passing landscape. Mike was more than pleased when they arrived in Gizre but there was a lot of commotion going on people were shouting and screaming in the streets, Jack and Mike were taken to a house, once they were safely inside, the house was then surrounded by armed men, Jack and Mike wondered whether they were now prisoners or if they were being heavily guarded for a reason. A while later the interpreter Abi arrived to let them know what was going on, he told them that the Iraqi's had wiped out one of their villages with chemical weapons there were hundreds of men's, women's and children's bodies lying in the streets looking like they'd been frozen on the spot in mid movement. There were PKK troops all over the place, Jack and Mike were taken to another building that had a bomb shelter; on the way there they could hear the sound of heavy artillery firing in the distance. 'What the fuck's going on?' Mike shouted to Jack.

'I don't know, but I don't like the sound of any of this bollocks.'
'Me neither, do you think there's any chance of us heading back to Istanbul today?' 'More chance of going to hell.' Jack shouted.
'Just my fucking luck.' Mike moaned.
'Let's just concentrate on staying alive for now.' Jack said sternly. 'I'll second that.' Mike added.
The noise of the heavy artillery could be heard throughout the night. Jack drifted in and out of a disturbed sleep; but the unwell Mike found it to uncomfortable to sleep. Jack was woken from one of his sleeping spells by a huge explosion that shook the building. Jack sprang to his feet as pieces of the building fell all around him. 'Some fucking bomb shelter.' Jack shouted to Mike.
'We might be better off outside.' Shouted Mike.
'Fuck that, at least we've got some cover in here, and we don't know who is fuckin who out there.'
'Yeah, I suppose you've got a point.'
The two men put a few steel framed beds and some of the other sparse bits of furniture together to make a shelter within a shelter.
'What are we going to do now?' enquired Mike.
'Well me, I'm going back to sleep.' Jack said has he rolled himself under the makeshift framework.

The next morning the interpreter Abi woke Jack by prodding him with the barrel of a rifle.
'What the fuck, Jack shouted, as he rolled from his bed, don't point that fucking thing.' Jack shouted as he clambered to his feet.
Ali explained that they would have to move from their position but he didn't explain why. As Jack and Mike surfaced they noticed that most of the houses around them had been reduced to rubble during the night.
'What the fuck's happened here Jack?' Mike gasped as he viewed the destruction. 'Could be worse mate, it could have been us.'
The interpreter called to the two men to follow him, which they did, they were told to get into a truck with some tribesmen which they did there were several trucks in a row, they left in a convoy, the two men were puzzled as they had no idea where they were going to find themselves next, they tried to ask Abi the interpreter but he said that he had no idea either. It wasn't long before they came across more troops and hospital tents full of injured, dying or dead men. The heat was horrendous the hospital tents full of mosquitoes the whole place stunk of death and fear, there was little sanitation, little food and no clean water, the sound of large artillery fire in the distance was ever present. 'How the hell did we get here?' asked Mike.

'I think we've died and gone to hell.' Was Jack's answer.
'It looks like it too.' Mike pondered.
'I only came to look at a painting.' Jack quipped.
'I think we should give it a miss and get out of here.'
'How the fuck are we going to do that?' Jack quizzed.
'Ask that Abi feller.' [y]
Jack asked Abi what was happening and how could they get out of there as quickly as possible, Abi explained that because there was a problem with Iraq all available troops had been sent to the border, unfortunately for Jack and Mike because it would not have been safe to leave them in Gizre the local PKK leader had decided to take them with his troops to the border. Later that evening there was a loud cracking noise across the skyline everyone looked up to see what was happening, within seconds the bombers had emptied their loads across both sides of the border, there was panic everywhere as troops and civilians tried to find some cover, within seconds the raid was over the roaring planes disappeared into the darkness from whence they came the loudness now gone and the silence only broken by the screams of the injured as they cried out for help in the darkness. Jack who had taken cover under the convoy of trucks crawled over to where Mike

was lying. Jack loudly whispered to Mike but got no response, he crawled closer and shook Mike's arm, there was still no response, Jack rolled Mike over onto his back, he knew straight away that he was dead, he felt wetness on his hands and realised that it was blood from a wound in mikes head, Jack crawled back out from under the truck and went in search of Abi. Jack found Abi and explained to him that Mike was dead. 'I am very sorry,' he repeated several times.
'Fuckin Iraqi's.' Jack shouted.
'No.' said Abi shaking his head.
'What do you mean no?'
'Not Iraqi planes.'
'Well whose planes then?'
'American.'
'Fuckin American.'
'Yes American. they always miss the target.'
'Oh, I know the yanks they just bomb everything in their path and hope for the best.'
'This happens a lot on this border, they've killed more of our troops than the enemy.'
'That figures.' Jack replied.
'When the morning comes we bury your friend, yes?'
'If we get the chance Abi, only if we get the chance.
At first daylight the scene of devastation was unveiled, many of the tribesmen were injured or dead, four of the trucks had been blown to

pieces and what was now left of them was debris just lumps of rusting metal torn and twisted, to be left in the desert sands for the rest of time. Jack went over to where Mike's body had lay for the past few hours, he looked at the damage to the head wound that had killed him, Jack thought it must have been a flying piece of shrapnel that had prematurely erased his life. When Abi arrived back on the scene Jack recruited him to help him to carry Mike's body to a ditch that he'd found some two hundred yards away, the two men lowered Mike into the ditch covered him with some rags that Abi had found then covered the body over with rocks, they couldn't dig a grave even if they wanted to as the ground was far to hard, they made a makeshift cross and Jack wrote on it; Mike Kalowski killed by friendly fire, you can count on America, after the makeshift funeral Jack followed Abi around for a few hours while he tried to find out who was now in command, luckily for Jack it was to be the same leader as before has he had survived the night before's onslaught and along with some of his men was trying to set up a new command post. It took two days to get organised and to move all the bodies; an old fashioned digging machine had been brought in from Gizre to dig a mass grave to cater for all the dead and to push all the now scrap vehicles into a protective barrier around the new command post. The following day Abi was asked if he could drive one of the trucks as the command needed to send a message back to Gizre, he explained that he couldn't drive but when he told Jack what had been said, he sent Abi back to the command post to explain that Jack could drive the truck and Abi would go with him to pass on the messages. It didn't take them long to get back to Gizre another place that Jack had seen devastated in the previous few days, they both stayed the night with Abi's friends arising early the next morning. Abi wanted Jack to drive him back to the frontline to join his leader whereas Jack was demanding that Abi go with him to Istanbul. Jack had to use psychology regarding the treasures and bribe him by giving him his watch to get him to return with him to Istanbul the first hour or so was used up by begging enough fuel for the trip to Istanbul; Jack was so pleased when he eventually got underway and although he didn't say anything to Abi his own thoughts were that he would not be returning to this god forsaken place ever again, as far as Jack was concerned Sean could stick his fifteen million dollars where the sun don't shine. Jack showered and then lay on his bed wrapped in towels when he fell asleep, he was in a deep sleep when he dreamt that his body was being kissed all over he stirred a little as his dream went on, his body was being teased and tantalised he had a huge erection that was about to explode then

suddenly he woke up 'What the fuck are you doing here?' he screeched to the naked Maria.
'What does it look like?'
'Well it doesn't look good, what if Pat walks in?'
Maria carried on massaging Jack's erect penis and Jack who thought he'd been having a horny dream was on the point of exploding, the pressure was past the point of no return and Maria must have known it for in one swift move she swooped down onto Jack's throbbing cock and in two deep throat movements Jack exploded deep into her soft succulent still gently sucking mouth, Maria looked up at the now satisfied Jack and gently she sucked and licked him as he fell back to sleep. The next morning Jack went down to the restaurant for breakfast Maria and Pat were both there laughing and joking, Jack sat at their table, 'I had an amazing dream last night.' Jack said as he stared at Maria's huge breasts 'Did you now?' She answered with a question. 'Is Mike coming down for breakfast?' Pat butted in.
'No.' said Jack now shocked back to reality.
'What do you mean, no?' Pat snapped.
'The deals off folks.'
'What do you mean the deals off, our people have invested a fortune in this deal, we can't just walk away now, we've got people flying back and to from the states plus all our expenses,

hotels, travel everything our people have picked up the bill for all the groundwork, we can't pull out now.' Pat ranted.
Maria just sat there gob smacked as Jack added, 'Mikes dead the jobs gone boss eyed and I'm out of here rapido.'
'Mike's dead.' they both said in unison.
'That's right.' Jack replied.
How did that happen?' Pat asked choking on the words.
'I'll tell you what happened when we got down to Gizre the Iraqi's had gassed one of their border villages, me and Mike got caught up in the mayhem but we survived that and the heavy artillery that was rained upon us all through the night, then the next morning we got caught up in the mayhem again and finished up on the border on the front line with big fuck off shells flying back and to all day and night and on the last night that I was there the yanks flew over probably intending to bomb the Iraqi heavy artillery but the mad bastards bombed everything in sight including our command post, when the bombing had stopped, I went to make sure that Mike was okay but he was dead, killed by flying shrapnel I think, in the morning me and Abi buried him the best that we could. And not only is that the end of this story it's the end of this job for me, first chance I'm out of here. 'In a hell hole like this full of murderous and fanatical scumbags and he was killed by his

own people' Pat raved.
'So much for friendly fire.' Jack said. The three of them stared at each other in disbelief of these unexpected events.

Chapter Eight

Jack arrived back at Manchester Airport tired and unhappy at having wasted vast amounts of time and money on what had turned out to be a fruitless task. Charles was waiting outside and as Jack walked out of the building towards the taxi rank Charles pulled forward and pressed his horn to let Jack know that he was there, Jack put his bag onto the back seat of Charles' car and then climbed into the passenger seat, without hesitation Charles pulled away and headed for the Motorway.
'Some guy called Soapy keeps ringing for you Jack.'
'I'll get back to him as soon as I've recovered from this trip.' 'That bad eh?'
'You don't want to know.'
'Yeah, you're probably right.'
Charles dropped Jack off at home then went back to work at his fencing business which he'd started after Jack had sold the skip business and yard together with some worthless land in Portugal a few years before to the extremely devious slippery Sam Edwards. Jack on the other hand was just glad to get home alive from this last precarious adventure that had seen him risk life and limb for no good reason at all. Jack

collapsed into his armchair while Sandra put the kettle on to make him a brew, there was no doubt in Jack's mind that he was approaching burnout, he was drained, every muscle in his body was aching, all Jack wanted to do at that moment in time was to go to bed and sleep forever. By the time that Sandra came back with Jack's cup of tea, he was fast asleep, she thought about waking him but instead she took off his shoes and put a duvet over him, he slept through the night but he must have woken at least once she thought as she came down the stairs to see that he had moved from his armchair onto the settee, she made some breakfast before she woke him. 'What's going on?' he shouted as he was woken by Sandra shaking his shoulder.
'I've done you some breakfast.'
'I'm to tired.' He mumbled pulling the duvet over his head. 'Come out of there Dunkerley.' She teased.
The now awoken Jack poked his head out of the warm comfortable duvet his eyes squinted at the brightness of the morning light; he rubbed them for a second or two until he became accustomed to the brightness. 'I'll chance that cup of tea now hon.' He shouted to Sandra who had disappeared into the kitchen. 'It's on the table with your breakfast going cold.' She shouted back. Jack forced himself from the comfortable settee and made his way to the kitchen. 'Still tired hon?' she asked. 'Knackered.' Jack

replied.
'Well after you've eaten, you can go to bed for a while.' 'Not much chance of that I've got things to do.'
'Men.' She muttered.
'Man.' He answered.
'Yeah, something like that.' She pondered.
After finishing his breakfast Jack went for a drive to find a suitable public telephone, so that he could telephone Sean to let him know what had happened in Kurdistan, Sean had already heard the news or at least a part of it, he said that they would have to meet up sometime so that Jack could explain the full story to him, he invited Jack over to Ireland but Jack said that he was busy with other things and that he would meet up with him the next time that he came over to England. The telephone beeped for more coins as Sean agreed but before he could say any more the line went dead. Jack tried telephoning Pete again but still with no success, Jack didn't realise that Pete wouldn't be back for another week. Pete and Jane had taken a cancellation flight to Johannesburg in South Africa, Pete couldn't wait to get back and tell Jack about a man that he'd met there; Ray Brown was an ex salusi scout with the Rhodesian special forces before Rhodesia got independence in nineteen eighty Ray was a man with many stories to tell and he captured Pete's imagination with many of them as they passed

the hours away drinking and chatting on the hot moonlit nights, he told Pete that after Mugabe took over many of the salusi scouts and Rhodesian light infantry had gone to South Africa to work for the South African Government working as security advisors, security guards, policemen and mercenaries, Ray had crossed the seventy ninth parallel many times doing his nightly reccy's into communist Angola searching for terrorists there were an average of one hundred and fifty thousand communist troops on the border of Namibia and communist Angola made up of troops from Cuba, Russia, East Germany and others. Ray had safely crossed their lines many times to meet up with members from UNITA who were trying to fight the communists from within their own country, Ray and his men used to meet up with members from UNITA to carry out attacks on training camps run by the ANC and SWAPO; It was a matter of fact that Ray had come across many weird and wonderful sights during his nightly incursions into these strange and unwelcoming lands, one of the stories that made Pete's ears prick up was when Ray mentioned being involved in diamond deals in a place called Windhoek. Pete had thought from their first meeting that this was the type of guy that Jack would be able to do some business with he was obviously well informed and seemed more than capable of doing the things that he said he had done and although now not as young as he'd like to be he had kept himself in good condition. Before leaving South Africa Pete would make sure that he had Ray's details so that if it became necessary he would be able to trace him at some later date. Pete was confident that Jack would find a use for or from this unusual man. Jack however was wracking his brain about what to do next, the Cannabis job had collapsed due to there being no profit left in the business, the cig smuggling scam was apparently still ongoing but it was going to be spasmodic at the absolute best, the Irish, American, Turkish, Kurdistan deal had all but collapsed in tragic and unforeseen circumstances leaving Jack with no interest in resuming the deal at a later date even if the dust did settle in that region, the only way that Jack would be interested in opening that deal again would be if the Turks brought the goods to him and Jack knew that the chance of that was more than unlikely. Jack went to his car where he had left his mobile phone, he found that he had missed several calls, only four of them had left their own numbers where Jack could call them back, which he did, three of the four calls from Roger, Angel and Mohammed all were looking for the next cig delivery but Jack didn't have any answers for them at this time, he said that he'd let them know as soon as he knew anything himself, the fourth call however was from

Soapy who wanted to set up a meeting with Jack,
Jack explained to Soapy where to meet him, he'd told him where to get off the M6 Motorway where he would then be on the main Manchester road then by driving towards the town for about a mile he would see on the right hand side of the road the Rope and Anchor public house, `ring me when you get there' he'd told the big Scotsman. It was several hours later when Jack pulled onto the Rope and Anchor car park. Jack got out of his car and walked across the car park towards the bar he was distracted from his thoughts by the sound of a car horn beeping lightly, Jack turned his head to see where the sudden noise was coming from and as he did so a car on the other side of the car park flashed its headlights as to attract his attention, an arm protruded from the drivers window waving for Jack to go over, Jack stopped in his tracks he had been involved in many near misses on his life recently and even one on another pub car park just along the road from there, he didn't fancy the idea of actually volunteering to stand in front of any vehicle that could be used as a weapon against him. Jack stood his ground and just stared towards the car watching the protruding arm waving erratically, a couple of seconds later the arm went back inside the vehicle and Jack could see the window being wound up. The car door opened

and the big Scotsman stepped out onto the car park, shouting across the car park to Jack' 'Still fuckin paranoid you fuckin Sassenach.' 'I've got every fuckin right to be.' Jack shouted back. The two men met half way across the car park where they shook hands, then turning towards the bar they walked together chatting as they went. They sat in the corner of the very small bar area keeping their voices very low as they spoke to each other trying to avoid being overheard by any would be listeners. Soapy was still trying to trace the missing slippery Sam Edwards or Lord Lucan as Soapy now called him. Jack told him that he shouldn't have let him out of his sight when he had him the last time, although Soapy acknowledged that in retrospect Jack had been proved to be right, he thought that slippery Sam might have had the sense to realise his predicament and at least made some effort to pay his debt. Jack explained to Soapy that slippery Sam was a totally underhanded and devious character and in some quarters the line of thought was that Slippery was behind the murderous attempts on Jack's life. Soapy listened to what Jack had said and his reply was that if that was the case then why hadn't Jack gone after slippery Sam himself, in answer to that Jack had replied that he was having the same problem as Soapy as no one knew where the elusive and extremely dodgy character was hiding. Jack told Soapy that he would let him know if the missing man ever turned up. The two men left the public house together and after saying their goodbyes they walked back to their respective cars and a couple of minutes later they both left the car park. Jack with only a short drive before him would be home in no time at all; and Soapy with a long laborious drive back to Scotland ahead of him was not feeling to happy that his long journey had proved to be fruitless. Jack called into the Penny Ferry pub on his way home to see if anyone he knew in there had seen or heard of the elusive Sam's whereabouts, but once again the short journey had been wasted as no one had seen hide nor hair of the strangely elusive Slippery Sam Edwards and by all accounts no one in there had seen him for quite some time. The following day Jack rang Pete's phone again but once more there was no reply, he must have emigrated Jack thought to himself. A strange thought crossed Jack's mind and the thought was that there had been no strange cars following him or any attempts on his life while Pete was away, he wondered if there was any significance in that, but as quickly has it crossed his mind Jack discarded it, shaking his head as to why he'd even thought it in the first place. Jack having now recovered from his abortive mission into the wilds of Kurdistan was now feeling better within himself and ready to take on the world, he got into his car and went on his rounds to see if he could generate some business by visiting the movers and the shakers that he knew, the first stop was Angels house, Angel looked pleased to see Jack until Jack mentioned that he hadn't come with good news about the cigs, he explained to Angel that he was just on the mooch, bobbing and weaving on the look out for any good deals that might be in the offing. Angel thought about it for a few minutes then he said, 'Can you shift any shooters?'

'How many?'
'Loads.'
'What sort are they?'
'I'll find out if you're interested, someone offered them to me the other day but I didn't have a buyer so I knocked them back.'
'Where are they from?'
'I can't say.'
'I don't mean, who are they off, I mean what region of the world have they appeared from.'
'I'm not sure, ... I think that I heard the word Belgium mentioned.'
'Interesting, I might be able to do something with them depending on the price and what make they are.'
'I'll get onto it tomorrow.'
'Let me know the details as soon as you can, I'm not asking my man until I know that you can still get the bleedin things.'
Jack left Angels house and headed back home

to look through his address book to see if there was any other deals that he could put together. No sooner had he got to his front door when his mobile rang, it was Angel 'Jack is that you?'

'Yeah.'

'It's me can you come back?'

'When?'

'Now.'

'Why?'

'I've got some information for you on that deal we talked about.' 'See ya shortly then.'

Jack knocked on Angel's front door. 'You were quick.' He acknowledged.

'I can smell a shilling.'

'I know the feeling.' Angel laughed.

'So what's occurring?' Jack asked.

'Lots,' said the excited Angel, have a look at this for a shopping list.'

Jack looked at the list of weaponry that Angel had handed to him and upon the list was a multitude of arms from Belgian Fn's to Czech RAK's to Italian Berettas on top of that there was also C4 plastic explosive with remote detonators and boxes of hand grenades the list was interesting and varied. 'Before I make any enquiries, are you sure that these things can definitely be got hold of?'

'The man says so.'

'And that's all we can go on.' Jack sighed.

'What else?' Angel answered.

'Yeah, what else.' Jack said thoughtfully.
Angel gave the list to Jack, as he didn't want it to be left at his house in case it fell into the wrong hands. Jack left and went to find a public telephone box. 'Hello.' Jack said to someone as they answered the telephone.
'Hello, who's speaking please?'
'It's me, ...Jack from England.'
'Hello Jack, I didn't think that I'd be hearing off you for a while, after that last fuckin disaster.'
'Neither did I, but something's come up that may be of interest to you!' 'Okay, you've got my attention.'
'Before we continue this conversation, you'll need to come over here.'
'Why can't you come over here?'
'I've still not recovered from my last trip, and anyway this is for your benefit.'
'I'm sure that there will be a little benefit in it for you somewhere along the line Jack.' Sean laughed.
'I'm hoping for a little touch to get me over the weekend, the odd shilling maybe.' 'Okay, you've tantalised my taste buds, I'll be over in a few days, sooner if I can arrange it.'
'I'll wait for your call.' Jack said as he pressed the button that disconnected the call.
Jack was quite pleased that he hadn't been pressurised into having to go back over to Ireland, he didn't fancy being trapped in the

Bogside with the menacing Paddy's squeezing him into the back seat of their car or even worse the boot, after that last incident in Kurdistan especially as Sean's firm had picked up the bill for all the expenses, but then again Jack thought to himself, he was the one who'd taken all the personal risks and some of the risks had been extremely dangerous indeed and that danger had all been for nothing, Jack believed in his own mind that they were even if not ahead of the game as far has the bills were concerned; Jack was sure that he'd paid his share in blood, sweat and almost tears. Four more days passed and Sean had still not been in touch, maybe he's not going to ring at all Jack thought. Jack was shaken from his thoughts by his mobile phone bursting into life. 'Hello' Jack shouted. 'No need to shout.' Pete pleaded.
'Where are you?'
'I've just got home.'
'Thank fuck that you're back.'
'So you have missed me then.' Pete laughed.
'Behave yourself, Jack laughed, well maybe a bit.'
'I bet you've been having a right doss, while I've been away.' Pete chuckled.
'I wish.' Jack moaned.'
'Why what's been happenin?'
'I'll tell you when I see you.'
'And when will that be?'
'Today I hope.'

'Today Jack,......................... I've just got back.'
'We'll just meet for a quick chat, I've got a few things to tell you.'
'And I've got something to tell you Jack.'
'Sounds very interesting, I can't wait.'
'Shall we say the Duck at eight o'clock.'
'The Mucky it is Pete, see you then.' The phones clicked and the airwaves were silenced. The two men both arrived early, both excited at what the other had half said earlier on the telephone. They got some drinks then sat in the corner to chat, away from bored ears that may tune in to their conversation. Jack explained to Pete about him having to go back to Istanbul then on to Kurdistan where he got caught up in a war, then from there he finished up on the front line, together with an American that Sean had sent with Maria and Pat, he explained to Pete about the Americans bombing the wrong side of the border and Killing Mike with their friendly fire, Jack then had to find his own method to get back to Istanbul, then on returning home he was burnt out for a few days. Once he'd recovered from his ordeal, he'd chased a few deals here and there without any joy, but now there might be a deal in the offing with the Irish and some hardware that he'd come across while chasing a different deal.
'Well after that fiasco, I think my news might be a bit more easy on the ears.'
'That would be a blessing Pete.'

'Well Jack, I grabbed a last minute flight at the airport, and I finished up in Africa.'
'Africa.' Jack butted in.'
'Yeah Africa, Johannesburg actually, well I met this amazing character there called Ray Brown.'
'A proper African name that Pete.' Jack laughed.
'Yeah innit, anyway as I was saying I met this guy Ray Brown………..'
Pete went on to tell Jack about some of the wild and wonderful stories that he had heard from the lips of the now infamous Mr Brown. Jack's wandering mind soon moved into heavy concentration mode when Pete mentioned the word diamonds. Jack was seduced immediately by the idea of diamond smuggling in Africa; to him it seemed to be the epitome of every adventurers dream. Jack was definitely going to give this venture some serious thought. Pete having finished his tales of Africa and the amazing Mr Brown; made his excuses and went home to his beloved Jane. Jack left the pub a few minutes later, whereupon trying to drive off he realised that he had a flat tyre, he locked the car and walked back into the pub to ring a taxi, a few minutes later he returned to the doorway to await the arrival of the cab, he stood there for a few minutes when he noticed car headlights, he turned to see the car that was slowing down alongside him, Jack smiled as he walked

towards the vehicle and no sooner had he walked two steps forward when two shots rang out from the cars open rear window breaking the night's silence as it cracked the chilled air, Jack fell to the floor; he remembered nothing more about it until he was in the ambulance, sirens blazing, heading for the hospital. Half an hour later the sobbing Sandra rang Pete, 'Jack's been shot she screamed.'
'He can't be, I've just left him.'
'I'll have to go to the hospital, can you pick me up?'
'Yeah, sure, I'll be straight there.' The phones went down and Sandra put on her coat to await Pete's arrival. Pete raced towards the hospital disregarding all the rules of the road in his haste to get there. On arrival at the hospital Sandra tried to discover what had happened to Jack, but could only find out what she already knew, that he'd been shot and he was now in the operating theatre. An hour or so later when the doctor left the operating theatre he came to speak to Sandra to explain that Jack had been shot twice, once in the shoulder and once in the leg, he had also banged his head as he hit the ground causing a temporary concussion and leaving his head a little bruised, he told her that Jack would be okay, and Sandra sighed with relief. The doctor told her to go home and get some rest, as Jack had been given an anaesthetic and she wouldn't be able to speak

to him until the next day, but Sandra was adamant that she wanted to see him straight away to make sure in her own mind that he was okay before she left the hospital. She waited until he was moved from the operating theatre to a room on the ward, before sitting at his bedside for a while stroking his hand, her tear filled eyes releasing the occasional teardrop that would run down her soft cheeks before dropping off her chin into her lap, now and again she would wipe her cheeks with the tissue that she'd been holding tightly in her hand. She looked at Jack intently, wondering what was going on or what had he done to warrant such havoc being wreaked upon their lives; it was going to be a long night she thought, Pete came into the room and spent quite some time coaxing her to leave, she eventually gave in, vowing to return the next morning. As they left the room Sandra noticed the uniformed man sitting on a chair. 'What's he doing here Pete?' 'After that episode, when he was attacked in hospital before, I suppose it's necessary.'

'Yes it makes sense, but Jack won't like it.'
'You're not wrong there.'
Sandra and Pete walked together through the long maze of corridors until they eventually found the main exit. Pete drove Sandra home and dropped her off promising to return the next morning to take her back to the hospital. Sandra

however didn't wait for Pete's arrival she was up bright and early and drove herself to the hospital. Jack was already awake when Sandra arrived; he'd sat himself up in the metal framed bed and by folding the huge pillow in half, he propped himself up. Sandra immediately went off to find a nurse and returned a few minutes later with two more pillows, which she slotted behind him to make him more comfortable. A few minutes later Pete arrived complaining that he'd been looking for Sandra; several minutes later the same two detectives arrived who had questioned Jack before when he'd been attacked along with a nurse on a previous occasion.
'Fit enough to talk?' asked one of the detectives.
'Depends who to.' Jack croaked.
'Listen Jack we're here to help you.'
'That'll be a first.'
'Just tell us what you know about last night, and we'll be out of here.'
'I don't know anything.'
'Where've I heard that before, I wonder?'
'That's the truth.'
'So what do you remember?'
'I ordered a taxi, I went outside to wait for it, and then I woke up in here.'
'So you're telling us that you didn't see who shot you.'
'That's right.'
'What sort of car was it?'

'It was dark, the car was dark, I was shot, I banged my head and that's all I know.'
'This story is getting a bit repetitive Dunkerley.' Said the now angry cop. 'Repetitive but true.' Jack replied.
As the two detectives turned to leave the room, one them turned and said, 'We'll be back.'
'Arnie again.' Pete mocked.
One of the detectives turned and glared at Pete as he left the room.
'Strange thing with them coppers Pete, you tell em the truth and they still don't believe ya.' Jack mused.
'Truth or lies they don't know the difference coz they lie so much, they don't know which is which anymore.'
'They're all lying bastards Pete, every last fuckin one of them.'
'I know that Jack, I don't need to be told.'
'That's for sure.' Jack mumbled.
'Once the police had disappeared from sight Pete leaned over to where Jack was lay and whispered, 'Didn't you see who it was Jack?'
'Not a thing Pete, not a fuckin sausage.'
'Fuckinell Jack we've got to find out who it is before they get lucky.'
'Well they're having enough tries, they only have to get lucky once, and I've got to be lucky every time.'
'I think you've used up all your nine lives already, you'll have to keep your head down.'

'That's easier said than done.'
'Why?'
Because who do I keep my head down from?'
'It's not going to be easy.'
'Well at least you understand that much.'
Sandra had to go home to sort out the children who were now staying with her mother, Sandra still had to go home and sort out their clean clothes and organise their activities and help with the cooking of their food whenever she could, no matter what happened to her or Jack life still had to go on for the children sake. Two hours later Sandra returned to the hospital, Pete had already left when Sandra got back; he told Jack that he'd call back later when he'd eaten.
'Someone rang for you while I was at home.'
'Who?'
'Someone called Sean, he sounded Irish.'
'There'll be a good reason for that, he is Irish.'
'Funny bar steward, she growled, anyway I told him where you are, and he wants to come and see you.'
'No, Jack shouted, tell him not to come here, there's too many of the odd-lot about.'
'Okay, he says he'll ring back tomorrow, when he does I'll tell him.' 'Which phone did he ring on?'
'Your mobile, why?'
'Just wondered, that's all.'
The following day when Sean phoned Jack's mobile and Sandra answered, she explained to Sean about the possibilities of the odd-lot being

about and the fact that there was at least one uniformed odd-lot guarding the door, checking peoples I.D. even the doctors if they tried to enter Jack's room. Two days later Jack's solicitor went to enter Jack's room when the policeman guarding the room stopped him from going in, the guard checked the solicitors I.D. before letting him pass saying 'Sorry to have troubled you Mr Marno, then opening Jack's door for the solicitor, he shouted to Jack 'Your solicitors here.' The policeman closed the door after the solicitor walked in. Jack who had been sleeping opened his eyes a little, then on seeing who it was his eyes flashed wide open as he sat bolt upright in bed. 'How the fuck did you get in here.' He shouted. 'Shush.' said the man pointing his finger at his lips.

'How did you get past the cop?'
'Just got to have the right look and the right I.D., said the suited man as he threw the false I.D. on the bed for Jack to look at.
'Fuckinell, Jack said, you could've been anyone.'
'Your security is shit Jack.' Sean snapped.
'I can see that.' Jack moaned.

Sean offered to help Jack to deal with the problem that he was having, but when he found out from Jack that he had no idea where the attacks were coming from, he said that with nothing to go on it was an impossible task, but he would be willing to help if Jack ever

discovered who his attacker was. They also discussed the Kurdistan disaster and the loss of Sean's American friend Mike. Sean was pleased that Jack had at least buried Mike's body and given him some sort of a funeral. The two men then discussed the real reason for Sean's visit to England, Sean was more than interested in the weaponry, Jack said that if Sean bought any of the tools then he would have to get them back to Ireland himself as he was unable to do that for him, Sean acknowledged Jack's honesty and replied that he had all the transport that was necessary to get anything that he needed back to Ireland. Sean wanted to know when Jack would be getting out of hospital, Jack's answer was that after Sean's easy breach of security, he would be leaving the next day even if he had to sign himself out of the place. Sean said that he would stay a few days so that he could view the weaponry. Jack promised to arrange a viewing of the goods as soon as he could. Sean got up off the chair, picked up his false I.D. off the bed and prepared to leave, as he did so Sandra opened the door and started to enter the room, she stopped in her tracks for a second when she saw the man, but he just continued past her and walked out of the door shouting goodbye as he left. 'See you Sean.' Jack shouted. The policeman bobbed his head around the door and said, 'I thought his name was Gary?'
'It is.' Spluttered Jack.

The policeman added nothing more; he just closed the door.
'Was that the Sean who rang me the other day?' Sandra whispered. 'Sure was.' Jack smiled.
'Well he seems a bit impatient to see you.'
'He's only here for a few days, and then he's off again.'
'You won't be out of here by then.'
'Oh, I will.'
'What do you mean?'
'I mean if Sean can get in here that easy then it won't need much imagination for whoever's having a go at me to come up with the same type of idea.' 'I suppose you're right, we'll have to get you out of here.' 'Well it's a bit late tonight; we'll sort it in the morning.

The next morning around ten o'clock a paramedic approached the reception desk in the entrance hall of the hospital, he asked the receptionist if she could tell him which room or ward Mr Jack Dunkerley was on, he was stunned when he was told that Jack Dunkerley had gone home earlier that morning, as the paramedic walked away from the reception desk, the receptionist turned to one of her colleagues and said 'I've never seen him around here before.'
'No neither have I ...he must be new.'
Jack hobbled in to his front room and collapsed himself into his comfortable armchair 'It's good to be home.' He shouted to Sandra who was

walking towards the kitchen to make them both some breakfast. 'It's good to have you home.' She smiled. After breakfast Jack phoned Pete. 'I'm home Pete, can you call round for a chat?'
'I've just got up mate; I'll be about an hour.'
'There's no rush, I'm not going anywhere.'
As soon as the phones went off Pete jumped out of bed and headed for the shower to wake himself up, after showering he made some tea and toast, he drank half of the cup of tea and a slice of toast, he took the rest of the toast with him into the car to eat has he drove to Jack's house. The red faced spluttering Pete banged on Jack's door; Sandra wondering what the urgency of the knocker was, she rushed to the door and opened it to the spluttering Pete and said, 'What's up Pete?' Pete tried to talk but he was glowing red faced and choking and pointing to his mouth, Sandra on realising what was happening started to slap him on his back as Pete stumbled into the house, Jack wondering what all the commotion was about, struggled from his armchair towards the hallway, where he found the now blue faced Pete on his knees choking, Jack moved forward as quickly as he could, pushing Sandra out of the way he got behind Pete and punched him with two heavy blows into his back, the problem blocking Pete's airways exited his mouth and he caught the lump of half chewed toast in his hand, Pete was gasping for air but at least he was now

breathing. 'Are you okay Pete?' Jack asked.
'Yeah, I'll be alright now.' He gasped.
Jack and Sandra helped to lift him back on to his feet, as the two men went through to the lounge to sit down Sandra went to fetch a glass of water for Pete, when she returned with the water Pete was telling Jack the story about what had happened to him, Pete had been eating his breakfast as he drove over to Jack's house when just as he turned into Jack's street some stupid woman as he called her reversed out of her drive right in front of him causing him to slam his brakes on, and at which time he was thrown forward only being stopped by the fact that he was wearing a seat belt, it was at this time that he got the toast stuck in his throat, he realised that he was in trouble, so he waved at the woman to attract her attention for help but she just waved back at him and drove off, by this time he was starting to panic so he accelerated the other fifty yards up the road to Jack's house and banged on the door and the rest his history he concluded. 'Well now that you've recovered, we'll get down to business.' 'Business Jack, Pete half shouted, I think that we should be looking for whoever it is taking shots at you.'
'And where would we start Pete?'
'I don't know.'
'And neither do I, so until we get some information in that direction, we'll have to crack on with other things.'

'Like what?'
'Sean is still over here for a day or two and he wants to see the existence of some weaponry.'
'Do you want me to collect it and bring it here?'
'Do I fuck, you fuckin lunatic.'
'So how do we do it then?'
'You'll have to drive me to a couple of places Pete, I won't be able to drive for a few days yet, so if you stay off the toast we'll be alright.' Jack laughed.
'Jack you can't go gallivanting about, you've just got out of hospital.' Sandra complained.
'I'm not doing much and as soon as everything's sorted, I'm due for a rest maybe we can get away for a few days with the kids.'
'See what the doctor says when you've had your stitches out.' 'Maybe you're right, we'll see eh?' Sandra helped Jack to put his coat on; he could only put one arm through the sleeve as the bullet that had pierced his shoulder restricted the movement of his other arm. Pete adjusted the passenger seat in his car so that Jack could get in and out easily. As soon as Jack was comfortably seated in Pete's car the two men set off on their travels. Angel had taken possession of the weapons and had stashed them at a farm belonging to a friend of his, Jack and Pete followed Angels car through the winding country roads until they reached the quiet farm.

Angel got out of his car and walked to one of the outbuildings, which he unlocked, he went in and looked around then went back to the door and waved across to Jack and Pete, inviting them to come into the building. Pete walked, Jack hobbled the few yards to the building, it was dark and dank, Angel eventually found a light switch and there before their very eyes was a terrorists dream, there were guns and hand grenades, rocket launchers, and boxes of ammunition and plastic explosives; 'Did you get a price list?' asked Jack.
'Yes.' replied Angel as he took it from his pocket and handed it to Jack.
'I'll have to bring someone to see this stuff.' Jack stated.
Angel threw the key towards Jack shouting, 'Lock the place up when you leave and let me know as soon as the deal's done.'
'Okay.'
'Later then.' Angel shouted as he left, obviously in a hurry Jack thought as he heard the sound of screeching tyres as the Angels car pulled away. 'Right then Pete, let's get out of here.'
'Couldn't agree with you more.' Pete answered practically running for the door.
'Whoa slow down, there's no need to panic.' Jack shouted to him. By the time Jack got to the car Pete was seat belted in and the engine was running. 'Are you in a rush Pete?' Jack

asked.

'Only to get away from here.' Pete answered.

'We'll have to come back again later.' Jack added.

'Why?' Pete shrieked.

'We'll have to let Sean have a look at the goods.'

'Fuckinell Jack I'm going to have a bleedin heart attack.' 'Calm yourself Pete it's only a bit of business.'

'Not the sort of business that we're used to.'

'Maybe, but business is business, and we need the dosh.' 'I'm not sure that I need it this much.'

'You say that now, but when you're counting your share of the money, you'll be glad that you came.'

'And if I'm locked up, I'll be wishing that I hadn't.'

'Qui sera sera.' Jack said as they drove along looking for a telephone box.

Upon finding a public telephone box some miles away Jack rang Sean and said that he'd have to see him as quickly as possible, Sean said that he'd be down as soon as possible and he'd ring as soon as he was in the area. Pete and Jack went to a cafe to kill some time while waiting for Sean to arrive, it was two hours later when Sean rang to say that he was in the area. They arranged to meet near to the Motorway, which was in the right direction for where they needed to be. 'What's the panic

Jack?' Sean demanded. 'I've got those goodies for you to see.'

'Good, good, when can I see them?'

'Right now if you follow us.' Sean followed the two men along the narrow twisting lanes until they reached the farm, Jack got out of the car first and unlocked the door, he was followed into the building by the two other men, Sean now wearing surgical gloves soon got down to work inspecting the weapons, the other two men just stood and watched as he went through the many different boxes one after the other. 'Have you got a price list?' Sean asked.

Jack passed him the price list, not the one that Angel had given to him but a new one that he had revised while waiting in the cafe for Sean to arrive, the newly revised price list allowed a few extra shillings for Jack and Pete. Jack was thinking a little extra for himself to take on holiday and a little extra for Pete in case he needed a heart transplant when the one he had now packed in with the stress. Sean scanned the price list and then turning to Jack he said, 'I'll take the lot.'

'Fine with me.' Jack smiled.

'When can I take them?' Sean asked.

'There all yours, take them when you want' Jack said as he threw the key to Sean.

'Er right.' Sean uttered.

'Yeah right, we're off.' Jack said has he turned to head for the door, where Pete who didn't need

telling twice was already exiting the building.
'Thank fuck for that.' Pete said as they drove away.
'A bit uncomfortable for you Pete.'
'A bit is an understatement.' Said Pete wiping his sweaty forehead. 'Let's go home Pete.'
'Yes milady, Pete said doing his best Parker to Lady Penelope impersonation. Jack smiled and said, 'It's been a long week Pete.'
'Jack it's been a long fuckin year, it's time we retired.'
'Soon Pete, real soon.'
The following day the panicking Angel was on the phone to Jack 'Did you move that stuff?'
'No not yet.'
'We'll have to meet Jack it's important.'
'Okay, where and when.'
'Can you make it to the farm in about an hour.'
An hour later Angel pulled into the farmyard and parked next to the outbuildings, he waited a few minutes before getting out of the car and walking around to stretch his legs, he was getting anxious and the fact that Jack was late did not cheer him up. He had hardly taken a few steps when a voice bellowed out from behind some farm machinery. 'Armed police put your hands on your head.' Angel stood there looking about him, there were men running about all over the place, he looked up and saw men on the roof of the building aiming rifles at him, he put his hands on his

head, the rest of him was frozen on the spot. They pushed Angel towards the locked door of the outbuilding, they demanded the key from him, and when he said that he didn't have it, one of the policemen cracked him on the back of the head with the butt of his gun creating a small gash that immediately pumped blood through Angel's thick head of hair, and he could now feel the blood on his neck, The now un-amused Angel was getting angry, he had visions of steaming into some these bully boys, but soon realised that he would then become another statistic shot during his arrest and no witnesses to tell the tale. Another murder done by the police then justified later. The police searched him and searched his car looking for the key to the outbuilding, the sound of a car racing into the farmyard broke the monotony momentarily, Angel was hoping that it wasn't Jack and luckily it wasn't it was another police car that had come to join in the festivities.

'Okay break the door down.' One of the senior police shouted. Two other police returned from the boot of the recently arrived car carrying a battering ram, they smashed into the door of the outbuilding several times before it gave way to their brutality. The armed police ran into the empty building shouting and screaming, Angel assumed that they did this to hide the fact that they were all terrified, he knew that they were all shitbags on their own, they only liked to fight when the odds were fifty to one in their favour or they were all armed and were running into a house where there were unarmed people and their children, the British police are renowned for terrorising children, women and defenseless people. It seemed to Angel that you have to be a coward by nature to qualify for the job. He watched with some amusement as they played soldiers like they were in some Arnold Schwarzenegger movie, playing make believe. They were not so pleased when they searched the building and found absolutely nothing, not only were all the goods gone but whoever had been there had done a magnificent job of cleaning up before they left. They cut the plastic ties from Angels hands which had been put there instead of handcuffs, Angel immediately put his hand to the bump on his head which had been bleeding but which was now drying, he could feel his wet matted hair concealing the cut on his head. One of the senior police gave Angel a note to take to the council who they said would repair his door and pass the bill to them, they never mentioned what they were looking for or why they had bashed him on the head, it was as though it had never happened. Angel shakily drove away from the farmyard, he was steady for the first few hundred yards then his foot hit the gas big style, he practically flew home. Later in the evening after

arrangements had been made, Angel met up with Jack in the Mucky Duck. 'Where the fuck did you get to?' Angel demanded.
'Well lucky for us, Pete here was looking up in the sky at a fuckin kestrel, when we approached the farm he saw some men on the roof of the outbuildings with rifles, so we thought we'd give it a miss.'
'Thanks a fuckin lot, leave me to cop for the shit then.'
'It would have looked a lot worse if we'd turned up.'
'Suppose you're right.'
'What happened anyway and why aren't you locked up.'
Angel told them the story about what had happened at the farmyard, and how they'd bashed him on the head and then how his heart was thumping like he'd run a marathon when they smashed the door down, then low and behold the place was as clean as a whistle, and because there was nothing there, no crime, no evidence of a crime then the police would have to pay for the damage.
 'Okay, but forgetting all that for the moment, why were the fucking odd-lot there in the first place.' Jack demanded.
 'This guy who used to work for me, he's been nicked on some semi-serious charges, anyway he's rolled over and grassed loads of people up, I heard that he'd been nicked and what he was

up to off a solicitor friend of mine, anyways this guy knew that I used to stash my dodgy swag on the farm, in fact he used to take it up there for me sometimes, but I caught him nicking off me a couple of times, so I sacked him, now I suppose he sees this as a chance of getting his own back, and getting himself out of the shit at the same time.'
'Some nice people you employ?'
'Can't tell til they go boss-eyed can ya.'
'No, I suppose not.'
'The fuckin odd-lot would have thought they'd won the lottery if they'd gone up there the day before, fuckinell they only came looking for a bit of knock off.' 'Are you sure? .... there was a lot of firepower.' 'They always go over the top these days in case there's any kids about that they can frighten.'
'That figures, anyway what happened to the goods that were in there?'
'What do ya mean, I thought that you'd moved them.' 'No, not me.'
'What the fuck's going on Jack?'
'Hopefully Angel, my people will have taken them, but I've not spoken to anyone yet.'
'Well hurry up and speak to someone, I'm crappin meself here.'
Jack told him to wait where he was while he went to find a phone box, ten minutes later Jack returned with the news that the man he'd

been trying to get hold of had his phone turned off. The Angel looked petrified
'Fuckinell Jack, I hope that nothings gone wrong.'
'We'll have to wait and see tomorrow.'
'Tomorrow.' Angel moaned.
'Well we ain't gonna get any joy today with the phone turned off.'
'Suppose not, but I'm in the shit for a lot of money if this goes wrong.' Angel moaned again.
The following day Jack was up bright and early and in turn he got Pete out of bed and round to his house, as he still couldn't drive with his injuries. They drove away from Jack's house in search of a phone box, and then on finding a suitable place to use the phone Jack rang Sean.
'Where are you?' Jack asked.
'Back home.'
'That didn't take long.'
'No, I was only waiting to speak to you, I'd finished my other business over there.'
'Did your man sort the goodies out?'
'Have you not looked?'
'No, you've got the key.' Jack lied not wanting to let Sean know that he knew it was gone and not knowing who had taken it.
'Fuckinell, I told my man to leave it behind under a brick.'
'Maybe it's still there then?'
'Aye probably.'

'Is there anything left?'
'No, we've taken the lot, and we've cleaned up after us, not like the usual amateurs.' 'Good, thanks, when will I be seeing someone with the spondooleys, we've got to eat you know.'
'Give us a few days, and I'll have someone to see you.'
'Cheers mate, take care.'
The two men turned off their phones and Jack went back to Angel with the good news. Angel breathed a sigh of relief knowing that everything was under control and that he would be getting paid in the next few days. The next morning Jack had an unusual phone call, two brothers he knew from Doncaster, Sean and Tony Ryman, Jack hadn't heard off them for a couple of years, they were opening a nightclub and they wanted Jack to go up for the opening night, he said that he would go with Sandra, he took the address of the club and the date it would be opening, he said that he'd keep in touch, they said their goodbyes and he put his phone down. 'Funny old world.' Jack muttered to himself as he hobbled into his kitchen to make some tea. Later that morning Sandra drove Jack to the hospital to have his stitches removed. On the way back from the hospital Sandra pulled the car into a lay-by in front of a row of shops and parked the car. 'What are we doing here?' Jack asked.
'We're going in there.' She answered

pointing her finger towards the row of shops. 'Where?'
'There, in that travel agents.'
'Travel agents.' Jack spluttered.
'Yes, the travel agent's, remember what you said, about us going on holiday once you'd had your stitches out.'
'Well they're out, but they've not got as far as the bin yet.' Jack laughed.
'If I don't get you now it will all be forgotten, you'll be busy doing something else and then it'll be just wait a bit longer, then a bit longer until it's gone from all our minds.' 'For a change I think you're right.' He laughed.
Sandra smiled and said 'For a change eh?'
Jack struggled out of the car and hobbling along the pavement he followed Sandra into the travel agent's office, where Sandra with the help of Jack's credit card booked a two weeks holiday to Florida, it was a lot cheaper than it should have been as it was a holiday that someone else had cancelled and also because it was to be taken with only a couple of days notice. 'We'll never be ready in time.' Jack complained.
'Oh yes we will.' Sandra said confidently.
They drove home from the travel agents discussing what they were going to have to do over the next forty eight hours before it was time for them to leave, they would also have to make their way to London to catch the flight to Florida. It was going to be a mad rush for them

to be ready on time, but Sandra was determined to go away with Jack and the children, so they could spend some quality time together away from the rigours of their very day life, she felt that Jack needed a break from his stressful activities, although Jack wouldn't agree with her, Jack would much prefer to make enough money to be able to retire, which to him meant not taking holidays while there was work to be done. Two days after booking their Floridian holiday, Jack and his family boarded Virgins Boeing 757 aeroplane to begin their fortnight's holiday. Ten hours after leaving London's Heathrow airport Jack collected his hire car keys from the Avis desk, where they were waiting for him, Jack used one of the airports steel trolleys to carry his family's luggage down to the underground car park where the hire car was parked. Pete rang the doorbell and knocked on the door of Jack's house, but to no avail, He had only called at the house because Jack's mobile was turned off, and Pete had thought it to be rather odd, Pete looked through the windows and even climbed over the gate to look around the back of the house, where once again he peered through the windows into the empty house. Pete drove to a phone box. 'Hello Angel.'
'Hello, who's that?'
'It's Pete, Jack's mate.'
'Yeah, I know who you are, what's happening?'

'I was about to ask you the same thing.'
'What do you mean?'
'Have you seen Jack?'
'No,   why what's up?'
'I can't find him.'
'I don't want to hear this; my heart won't take it, the stress ….He mumbled.
'He'll probably turn up.' Pete smiled.
'Probably.' Angel spluttered.
'Alive as well, I hope.' Pete jested.
'It gets worse.' Said the now feeling unwell Angel.
'I'll let you know as soon as I hear off him.'
'Yeah, straight away.'
'Don't worry everything will be fine.' said the hopeful Pete.
'I've got some very heavy people, waiting for their dough off me, and that's dependent on Jack turning up, I've told them that they'll get paid today.'
'I'll get him to ring you as soon as he surfaces.'
'Yeah, yeah, thanks.' The phone bleeped for more money which Pete didn't put in, a second or two later the line was dead.
Pete went to a few places looking for Jack, before eventually finding himself at Jack's brothers house; Charles answered the door.
'Come in Pete, how ya doing?'
'I'm fine, I've been runnin around looking for Jack.'

'Looking for Jack! ...... Jack's not here.'
'What do ya mean? He's not here.'
'He's in Florida.'
'Fuckin Florida, what's he doing in Florida?'
'He's on holiday.'
'Oh, fuckin marvellous, there's all kinds of things going on, and he's on holiday, without telling a soul, fuckin marvellous.'
'Well he told me, I suppose he had to as I dropped them at Manchester airport, so they could get a flight to Heathrow. I've got his house keys in case of emergencies.'
'He never said a word to me.'
'It was a last minute thing, Sandra organised it, and to be honest Pete, I think that he needed to get away for a while with all these attacks on him from God knows who.' 'Yeah, you're probably right Charles, I just wish that he'd told me.' 'You know what he's like, he'll remember in a day or two and give you a ring.' 'Yeah, you're probably right.'
'If not, he'll be back in a couple of weeks.'
'It's not a problem, I'm okay, but there's a few others, one in particular who'll be panicking.' Pete grinned.
Charles walked Pete back to his car chatting has they went. Angel was ringing around trying to find Jack's whereabouts, he was under pressure to pay for the weapons and he couldn't raise the money until Jack had paid him. Sean had also tried to make contact with Jack without success;

Sean quickly arrived at the conclusion that Jack would contact him when he was ready. Jack by now had put all his worries out of his mind; he was determined to have a good holiday with Sandra and their children. They spent their first few days doing the tourist thing, visiting Disney land, Marine world, and the film studios, they even took a trip on an airboat into the Everglades, life was feeling good for Jack and his family until a couple of days before they were due to go home, they had been driving around sightseeing, when they stopped at a burger bar on the outskirts of Dade county, where they got something to eat, Jack and Sandra sat at a table underneath a parasol to keep the sun off them while they ate some lunch of burgers, fries and coca cola, the children were playing in a play area, when one of the children let out a scream causing Jack to go and investigate, when he got to the play area he could see that his kids and others were being bullied by a gang of eight Hispanic kids aged around twelve to fourteen years old; they had been asking the tourists for money and even taking the burgers off some of them; Jack went over and tried to get them to leave the play area and leave the kids alone, they just jeered and shouted abuse to him in Spanish, they thought that bullying kids was a joke, but Jack didn't like it; he took his two youngest kids by their hands and after screaming some abuse back at the bullying teenagers in English and broken Spanish

he walked off towards where he had been sat, he was half way back to his table when two cracks ringing out broke the carnival mood, the sound of a gun going off caused mass hysteria as men, women, and children ran for cover, Jack's children ran screaming back to their mother as Jack's crumpled body lay slumped on the floor bleeding. The teenage gang scattered in different directions getting themselves lost in the crowd during the panic. The next morning Jack was sat up in the hospital bed when Sandra and his family arrived to see him. 'I didn't expect you to be awake?' Sandra questioned.
'Well here I am, alive and well.' Jack jested.
'It's not funny Jack, you could have been killed.'
'But I wasn't San, and that's what matters.'
'You're right, but I thought you were dead when they took you away.'
'Apparently one of the bullets just glanced off my head knocking me out, not quite so lucky with the other one, it's caused a bit of leakage, and I've lost a bit of blood.'
'Will you be able to get the flight home tomorrow?'
'I don't see why not.'
'I hope so Jack, I don't want to spend another minute here.'
'You shouldn't complain it's been a good holiday.'
 'It's been ruined by this, a great holiday

ruined.'
'You can't blame the place, just a few little kids who've watched too much tele.'
'A few little kids with a big gun Jack.'
'I don't think that they knew what they were doing.'
'They've not done a bad job for amateurs.'
'They missed my main organs.'
'Oh lucky you.'
'Well I'm still alive.'
'No thanks to them Jack, and what if they'd hurt one our kids.'
'Thankfully they didn't.'
'Not physically, but what about mentally, they saw their Dad get shot and lying in the road bleeding and unconscious, they thought you were dead, they cried all night.'
'Well I'm okay now, so no need to worry.'
'Jack, no one can have this much bad luck.'
'I'd say it was good luck, if it was bad, I'd be dead.'
'Always the optimist eh hon?'
'I've got to be darling, I've got to be.'
Sandra and Jack spoke for a while longer until she had to dash off to organise the children and to pack their bags for the return flight the following day. The next day Sandra left the children in the hire car while she went into the hospital to collect Jack ready for the journey home. 'I've got a bit of a problem San.' Jack blurted.
'I don't like the sound of this.' She replied.

'They won't let me go.'
'Go, go where?'
'Home hon, they won't let me go home.'
'Why?'
'I don't know, I think it's the head wound, but I'm not sure.'
'We'll have to book into a hotel.'
'No you won't, you'll have to take the kids home.'
Sandra argued that she wasn't going home and leaving Jack there on his own, Jack talked her round by saying that it would be easier for him to get a flight back on his own in a few days time rather than trying to get a flight for all of them. Reluctantly she gave in and after getting Jack some clean clothes from the car, she drove to the airport where she parked the car and left the keys at the Avis office, she put herself, the bags, and the children into the lift, which took them from the car park to the departures lounge. She was not happy about leaving Jack behind; She did not like that idea one iota. Almost a day later Sandra and the children pushed the luggage trolley through the arrivals entrance of Manchester airport to be met by Charles who'd dropped them off there two weeks earlier. The children ran in front of the luggage trolley to greet their uncle Charles. 'Where's Jack?' he asked.
'He's not coming.' Sandra replied.
'What do you mean? He's not coming.'

Sandra went on to explain the events of the previous few days, and of how Jack came to be shot, and the fact that he would be following them home as soon as he could. Charles dropped Sandra and the children off at home before going to see Pete.
'What do you mean, he's been shot?' Pete screamed.
 'Like I said Pete, all my information is second hand.'
'He can't be shot, not again, fuckinell, he's been shot more times than John Wayne.'
'It's sure getting that way Pete.'
Pete volunteered to fly over to America to be with Jack, but Charles talked him out of it, by saying by the time Pete had got over there Jack could well be on his way home. After Charles had left Pete's house, Pete arranged to meet Angel, and Angel was extremely pleased to meet with him, he was almost glowing with anticipation at the thought that he was about to get paid off the weapons job. Unfortunately for the smiling Angel he had just taken a mouthful of beer when Pete blurted out the news about Jack having been shot. Angel emptied the once half swallowed beer all over the pubs table and carpet, choking, coughing and spluttering in the process. 'What do you mean, he's been shot.' Angel spluttered, now having visions of being shot himself. 'Like I said he's been shot and that's all I know.'

'Is he alive?' Angel pleaded.
'He was, the last time I heard anything.'
'Fuckinell' Angel complained.
'Everything'll get sorted out in the end.' Pete said.
'It'll be me that'll be getting sorted out if I don't pay for those tools.' Added Angel.
'Don't panic, things could be worse.'
'Only if I get tortured first.' Quipped the nervous Angel.
'Yeah, they might set about you with a liposuction machine, remove the fat from your belly, and pump it back into your dick.'
'I should be so lucky.'
'Then if they kill ya, at least you'll look good in the morgue.'
'Gee thanks, ya twat, you're a real comfort.'
'It's nothing.'
'Yeah, I know.'
Pete left Angel in the pub drowning his sorrows, he promised him that he would get in touch with him straight away if he heard anything from Jack, although the use of the word `if' did not cheer him up to much, his options were extremely limited. Like everyone else who was depending on Jack recovering, he would have to wait and see. Sandra answered the telephone it was Jack, they chatted for a while but he still didn't know when they would allow him to return home, he was waiting for a doctor to examine him as they spoke. Jack

promised Sandra that he would ring her later. That night however the telephone did not ring. Angel had rang Pete several times to ask if he'd heard anything, on getting no joy on his last call to Pete, Angel retired to bed for another restless night. Bright and early the next morning Pete's phone rang it was Ray Brown the Rhodesian guy that Pete had met in South Africa, he mentioned that he had a few things in the pipeline that might be of interest to Pete and his friends, Pete explained that he was tied up with a major project at the moment and he'd get back to him as soon as he could. Ray Brown offered his help if Pete needed it; Pete declined the offer but said he would keep it in mind for future reference. They said that they would be in touch with each other soon and at that they said their goodbyes, there was a click and the call was cut. The following afternoon a taxi pulled up outside Jack's house, the taxi driver got out of the vehicle and walked up the path whereupon he knocked on Jack's front door and waited for a few moments until Sandra opened it, 'I've not ordered a taxi.' She said looking past the man to the taxi parked in the road. 'No, it's not for you, I've got an injured man in the back, who needs a bit of help.' He was stopped in his tracks as Jack's head surfaced behind the vehicle as he managed to struggle out of the cab. 'Jack.' Sandra screamed as she raced out of their house towards her injured man, she threw her arms around him shouting, 'So this is why you didn't phone back?'

'I thought it would be a nice surprise.'

'It is, it is, come on I'll help you into the house.'

'Can you pay the cab fare, I've only got American dollars.'

'Let's get you into the house first, and then I'll have to find my purse.'

'Don't you know where it is?'

'I couldn't find it earlier.'

'I'll get a few quid out of the safe, to save the cab driver from waiting.'

'Slight problem there darling.'

'And what might that be hon?' he said.

'The safe key is in my purse.'

'It never rains but it pours, he said, do you think he'll take dollars?'

They just looked at each other and burst into laughter; there was always a funny side to everything, and no matter what happened they would always find it. Jack telephoned Pete, and told him that he was now back at home, Jack then asked Pete to call round to his house as quickly as he could, 'Bring some money with you.' Jack said before putting the phone down. A short time later Pete turned up at Jack's house, he rushed in through the open front door he was smiling broadly. 'It's good to see you Jack, how are you feeling?'

'Sore Pete, bleedin sore.'

'Well that can only be expected.'
'Did you bring some money with you?'
'Yeah.' Pete said as he pulled out a bag, and tipped the five grand out onto the table. 'What the fuck's that?' Jack asked.
'Money, you asked me to bring some money.'
'You're right, Jack laughed, but that might be a bit much.' 'Why what's it for?'
'Did you pass a taxi on the way in?'
'Yeah.'
'Can you nip outside and pay the driver?'
'Pay the taxi, you wanted money for a taxi?'
'Yeah, if you don't mind, and can you give him a tip, he's been out there a while.'
After Pete had paid the taxi driver and returned to the house, Jack explained the story to him about what had happened to him in Miami and the fact that the gunmen had just been kids, he also explained about the taxi fare and the fact that he only had dollars on him when he arrived back in England, and that when he had got home expecting Sandra to pay the cab fare, she couldn't find her purse, and he couldn't get into the safe because Sandra had left the safe key in her purse. Pete changed the subject by asking, 'How many more times are you going to get shot Jack?'
'I wish that I could answer that, it was my life's plan to never get shot at all.'
'Well it ain't fuckin working Jack.'
'You're not wrong Pete, but I've been lucky in a

way.'

'Lucky.' Pete blurted out.

'Yeah, I'm still here aren't I?'

'Only just Jack, you've had a lot of near misses lately and we need to get to the bottom of these attacks on you.'

'It would be handy Pete, but we're still in the same position as we were before, we don't have a clue.'

'We could do with capturing one of the attackers if it happens again, then torturing the bastard until he tells us who sent him.'

'Yeah, that would be really handy, but in reality it always happens when we're not expecting it, and then everything happens so fast that all plans go out of the window as self-preservation takes over.'

'I suppose you're right, it was just a thought.'

'A good thought too Pete, but like all good plans, reality kicks the shit out of them.'

Pete gathered the five grand up off the table and put it back into the bag that he'd brought it in, at that point Jack asked Pete to leave some money for him until he found the safe keys, Pete threw the bag of money with the five grand in it onto the table and said they'd sort it out later, Jack nodded in agreement. Pete mentioned that Ray brown the guy who he'd met in South Africa had rang him, Jack said that he'd like to meet the interesting Mr Brown once he himself had recovered from his recent injuries. Pete said that he would sort it out whenever Jack was ready; he did however explain to Jack that there were several matters nearer to home that needed dealing with, the first one of them being the settling of the account with Angel before he had a heart attack, Jack used Pete's phone to ring Sean and in coded language arranged for Pete to meet up with one of Sean's men the following day to collect the necessary funds. They also talked for a while about all the recent attacks upon Jack's person they also discussed the attack on Jack in Florida but Jack dismissed the idea that it was connected to the other attacks, he put it down to just a coincidence, Pete however wasn't absolutely sure and elected to keep an open mind. They discussed ideas that they both had about what was to be the way forward, for a quick killing and a fast exit back to the land of the retired, sipping cool drinks while sitting in the sunshine sounded a much better bet than being piss wet through in England and getting shot at to boot exclaimed the philosophic Pete. The two men agreed to meet the next day after Pete had been to see Angel to cross his palm with silver. Pete let himself out of Jack's house promising to return the next day after he'd met with Angel. After finishing his cup of tea, Sandra helped Jack up the stairs to their bedroom. 'It's been a long few days hon.' She remarked.

'Hasn't it just.' Jack replied as he collapsed onto

his warm comfortable bed. 'Let's see what tomorrow brings.' Sandra whispered.
'Will our luck change for the better.' He asked. Sandra grabbing the corner of the duvet and wrapping it around her head, and mimicking the voice of mystic Meg said, 'Tonight you are going to enter a warm and wonderful place, full of erotica and excitement before falling into a deep sleep.' 'If I don't have a heart attack first.' he laughed.
Sandra giggled from behind the duvet like a naughty schoolgirl. 'What a way to go.' she jested.
Beats being shot Jack thought, but found the words 'Yeah, you're right there.' Coming from his mouth. 'And tomorrow will be warm and sunny.' said mystic Meg. 'In England.' Jack blurted out laughing.
'In my heart.' said mystic Meg removing her duvet headscarf and smiling lovingly at Jack. Jack smiled back at her as she leaned forward to meet his lips, she helped Jack out of his clothes, then slipping out of her own, she kissed him again aggressively as she pulled the duvet over their naked bodies as they disappeared into a passionate embrace, their bodies writhing together in harmony, thrusting in unison towards a long awaited orgasm before collapsing breathless and sweating, the once all covering duvet dismissed to the floor as the two quivering bodies gasped for air and their

drained bodies lay silent and satisfied, any inhibitions now hidden by the cover of night. It was almost noon when Jack surfaced, he shouted down stairs to Sandra to put the kettle on while he took a quick shower, he'd hardly put the hot tea to his lips when his phone rang, it was Tony Ryman. 'Just checking to see if you're still coming tonight.'
'Tonight, ... what, sorry.' Jack mumbled.
'Tonight, just checking to see if you're still coming to our opening night.'
Jack quickly gathering his thoughts said, 'I'm sorry mate, but I've had a bit of an accident, what nights are you open, I'll call down as soon as I'm fit again?'
'Sorry to hear that Jack, Tony replied, get down whenever you can, we'll have a good night.'
'Yeah, I will, what nights are you open?'
'Four nights a week from Wednesday to Saturday, eight til late.'
'Okay mate, I'll be in touch.'
Jack turned the phone off and turning to Sandra he said 'Another night out we'll have to miss.'
'Why who was that?'
'The two brothers who invited us to the opening of their nightclub that I told you about, apparently it's tonight, and I said that I couldn't make it.'
'Me neither, I'm too tired now, so by tonight I'll be comatose,' she declared.
'I know the feeling, Jack smiled, and anyway

we can always go clubbing another time.'
'Yeah, when the kids have grown up, and
we're not so tired all the time.' Jack laughed
and said, 'By then we'll probably have given
up going to nightclubs.' 'There's always the
Derby and Joan.' She laughed.
'Bingo nights and lazy days.'
'If you can manage to stay alive long enough, we
might get to enjoy our old age.'
'I'm working on it.'
'You'd better be.'
She walked towards the kitchen, 'More tea Jack,
... Do you want anything to eat?'
'Some bacon wouldn't go amiss.' He called out.
'I'll see what I can muster.' She shouted back.
After a couple of cups of tea and a bacon
sandwich Jack was ready to take on the world,
or at least that's what he thought. After several
abortive calls Jack finally got through to Pete's
mobile phone. 'Is that you Pete?' Jack asked
through the crackly interference. He could just
make out that it was Pete, but he couldn't pick
out enough words to make any sense from what
he was saying. 'I can't hear you very well Pete,
so if you can hear me, call round to see me as
soon as you get the chance, there's no panic so
no need to rush.' It was gone teatime when Pete
finally arrived at Jack's house. 'Didn't you get
my message?'
'Yeah, hours ago.'
'And.'

'And you said there was no rush.'
'You wouldn't be taking the piss would you Pete?'
'No Jack, I wouldn't, and before you start getting on my case, it's been a long fuckin day.'
'Why, what have you been up to?'
'What have I been up to, I've been running about all over the show with some big fuckin paddy's collecting money from all and sundry, then they took me to a flat while they counted every fuckin last penny, then they gave me the money for the tools, then I had to go home and recount it all to make sure that it was right, I separated our money from Angels, then I travelled over to Angels house and paid him.'
'Is that all?' Jack jested.
'You're a cheeky bastard sometimes Jack.'
'Yeah, I know.' Jack laughed.
Pete smiled and mumbled something inaudible; Jack took no notice. 'How did Angel take the good news?'
'He was over the moon, he said thanks.'
'For the money?'
'No, for helping him to lose so much weight, he's lost about three stone.'
'He probably didn't have his wallet in his pocket when he got weighed.'
'Yeah, that's probably right.' Pete grinned.
'Well at least that's another deal done and dusted, what else is in the pipe line?' 'Thought

you'd never ask Jack, but this guy that I met in Africa is really interesting, we should go over there and meet him as soon as you're fit enough.' 'Sounds good to me Pete, but it'll be a while yet.'
'I know, but whenever you're ready.'
'Have we got any other deals that are only half done, anyone we've not paid or anything else that I've forgotten about?'
'Not that I can think of Jack.'
'I'm sure that someone will remind us if we've not paid them.'
'As long as it's not with a bullet.'
'You're so fuckin cheerful Pete.'
The two men went on to discuss other deals that may or may not happen, they chatted away in their own little world of dodgy deals and skulduggery well into the early hours, a constant source of nutrition supplied by Sandra, until eventually Pete looked at the time and on realising that the time on the clock was correct, he got up to go. Talk of this deal and that deal came and went over the next few weeks, nothing coming to fruition for one reason or another. Jack bored with the lack of deals going on and with nothing to get his teeth into declared, 'Pete we'll have a night out.'
'When.'
'Tonight.'
'Tonight Jack, it's fuckin Wednesday.'
'I know what day it is.'

'There's nowhere open.'
'I know just the place, it's quite a way off, so we'll leave early.'
A few hours later the two men pulled onto the car park of the latest new club to open in Doncaster. The two men dressed in their best attire approached the door of the club and went inside. There were several doormen stood around chatting, one of them welcomed them to the club, Jack paid the cashier and the two men walked through another door and entered the disco area, the brightly lit bar attracted the two men like moths to a light in the darkness. They ordered some drinks and as they waited Pete said, 'I can't spot any dolly's Jack.'
'It's dark in here Pete.'
'Not that dark.'
'Well it's early, they'll all roll in when the pubs shut.'
'Isn't it men that do that?'
'These day's I'm not sure.' They both laughed. When the barman returned with Pete's change, he looked him up and down, and then on passing the money to Pete, he looked straight at him and winked.'
Jack noticed, 'Something wrong with his eye Pete?'
'There fuckin will be in a minute.' Pete growled. Jack laughed.
Jack and Pete were shouting down each others ears, unable to communicate normally as the

music pounded, the flashing lights and smokey atmosphere another diversion to the normally focused pair. Jack felt a hand on his shoulder, he spun around quickly in order to surprise the would be attacker, but stopped in his tracks when he recognised the face of the man.
'You've not changed have you Jack?
'Hopefully not.' He smiled.
Jack introduced Pete to Tony; the two men shook hands. The three men struggled to have a conversation due to the loudness of the music, Tony waved for them to follow him, they went through a couple of doors and up some stairs to an office. 'Take a seat.' Tony offered. The two men sat themselves down in comfortable armchairs. Tony pressed a button on the console on his desk, as he did a huge pair of curtains opened to expose a large window through which most of the disco could be seen. 'That's fantastic.' Pete uttered. 'Can the people out there see in here? Jack asked.
'No chance of that, Tony laughed, it's two way mirrors.' 'It's a great view, but what time do the girls get here?'
Tony burst out laughing, 'I think you've picked the wrong night for girls Pete, Wednesday's is gay night.'
'Fuckin gay night.' Pete spluttered.
'Fuckin marvellous, Jack laughed, the one night we decide to go on the mooch and where do we end up ……..?'

'In a fuckin club full of willy woofters.' Pete butted in.

'It could be worse, at least you're out of town, and hopefully when you're leaving no-one will recognise ya.' Jack laughed.

'Being out of town in this case is a bonus.' Pete smiled.

'Unless of course there's someone here tonight who knows us?' Jack added.

'Don't say that Jack for fuck's sake, I'd never live it down, come on let's get out of here before the place fills up.'

Tony interrupted with 'No-one can see you in here, you can stay in here for a while I'll get some drinks and a meal sent up for you, we can have a bit of a chat about old times and maybe discuss some future ventures.'

'Sounds all right to me, what do you reckon Pete?'

'As long as I can sit down or keep my back to the wall.' He moaned.

'Behave yourself Pete, there's nowhere else to go, and it's pointless driving all the way back home now, we might as well enjoy Tony's hospitality, you never know what we might learn tonight.'

'I've learned something already.'

'What's that Pete?'

'Never to fuckin come here again on a Wednesday.'

'That's for sure.' Jack laughed.

Tony picked up the phone that was on his desk and dialed a number; he ordered drinks and some food to be delivered to his office. By the time the men had eaten their food and had a couple of drinks the club was packed with a multitude of men some obviously gay by their dress and their actions and others who were not so obvious, some dressed normal, and seemingly shy retiring types, others in their leather caps and cowboy chaps, pranced about flamboyantly, to Jack it was all rather amusing, a gaze into a world that not many straight people ever got to see, Pete however was one who didn't want to see it, he was by far to terrified of the whole scene. A very uncomfortable man Jack thought. Tony who was sat higher up at his desk asked Jack and Pete to stand up and look through the huge window, the two men stood up and walked towards the window. 'Over there at the end of the bar.' Tony pointed.
'Which end?' Jack asked.
'This end, this end near that post.' Again Tony pointed.
'Yeah, I've got the post, what about it.'
'The two guys to the left of the post.'
'Which two?'
'The two in all the leather gear and the studs.'
'Yeah, I've gottem.' Jack said casually.
'Two coppers them Jack.' Tony said while pointing again. 'Are you sure?'
'Course I'm sure, I've been watching them for

ages, trying to puzzle out where I knew them from, then it came to me, it was Phil Pearce's trial, I was sat in the public gallery for a few days watching the bastards, they're part of the national corruption squad one's called Porton and the other's called Harker.'

'Are they puff's?' Pete asked.

'Could be, Tony answered, but more than likely working under cover.'

'Why in here?' Jack asked.

'There's supposed to be a big ecstasy tablet organisation working the gay clubs, they'll be trying to find Mr Big.' Tony said thoughtfully.

'Find him in here.' Jack enquired.

'Not necessarily, they're probably trying to gather information.'

'Do you know many of these Gays Tony?'

'Well sort of.' Said the embarrassed looking man.

'I've got an idea, if you're up for a laugh.'

'As long as it doesn't come back on me.'

'It shouldn't Tony.' Jack smiled.

Tony listened intently to what Jack had to say before leaving the room, Tony gathered some of his gay friends together and told them the plot. The two leather-clad men standing near the post were approached by other gay men who asked them if they wanted to dance, the two men declined making believe that they were a couple, the two cops asked the men who had approached them, if they could get them any ecstasy tablets, they said that they couldn't at that time, but if they fancied going to a party after the club closed the local Mr Big was going to be there and he always had plenty of everything, they said they'd think about it and let them know later, they tried to find out where the party would be at but the men would only say that they'd take them there later, if they were interested. At the end of the night as club emptied the two leather clad cops approached the men who'd spoke to them earlier at the bar, and asked if the invitation the party was still on, a few minutes later they all piled into the back of a van and headed for the party. As they drove along the road bottles of beer were passed around and drank by the inhabitants of the vehicle, the cops not knowing that their specially prepared drinks had been spiked with Rohypnol. The gang of men arrived at the party in the rundown hotel, they parked the van and headed towards the sound of thumping music, there were already plenty of people mulling around outside, some of them dancing on the car park. The gang of men entered the building; it was a honeycomb of little rooms with short corridors running off a main corridor, one of the corridors led to a large room that in better days had been the function suite, the music was loud, the lighting was dim and the gang of men barged their way through the crowd to an area at the front near to where the old stage was located, it now housed the coked off his head

Disc Jockey, who was nodding his head up and down in time with the beat of the music, his glazed eyes in a trance like state, he hovered on his platform looking down into the sea of bodies that moved in rhythm to the throbbing beat, feeding his already over inflated ego to grand proportions. By now the two leather clad cops were far the worse for wear, they were almost on the point of collapse, they were taken along the corridor and put on beds in separate rooms, it wasn't long before the rumours ran rife among the crowd of gay men that there were two slightly pissed horny guys who were up for anything in rooms 212 and 213, it wasn't long before queues started to form along the short corridors leading to the men's rooms, the two leather clad men were soon stripped naked and led through a series of sexual activities, one after the other man after man entered the room and sexually abused the two men, there wasn't an orifice on their body that hadn't been subjected to some form of sexual treatment, the two sperm filled men oblivious to the goings on around them, the queues in the corridor seamlessly never ending as the two men's battered bodies were pounded throughout the night by a continuous flow of drug crazed men and sexual deviants; as the party came to a conclusion, the two men were moved to a different room and left. Porton waking in the darkness and thinking that he was at home put

his arm around what he thought was his wife, his battered body in pain at his every movement, his bed mate let out a loud manly snore jolting the half asleep Porton into the land of the living, 'What the fuck.' He screamed as he felt about in the darkness and found another man's cock in his hand. His scream caused the other man to wake. Porton found a light switch and turned it on, the two men looked around at the sparse room wondering where they were, they looked at each others bruised and battered bodies, they also had numerous love bites at all parts of their anatomies, they stared at each others bodies, Harker on realising what must have happened burst into tears, Porton stepped forward and put his arms around him, the two naked men stood in the room huddled together. Porton said, 'How am I going to explain these bites to my wife?' 'You'll have to tell her what's happened.' Harker replied 'Tell her what's happened, are you completely mad?'
'We'll have to tell someone.'
'If you ever mention this to a soul, I'll kill you myself.'
The two men walked slowly towards where their leather clothes were lay, they were sore as they moved, they both felt something that they thought was unsavoury leak from their rear orifice's and run down their leg's as they walked across the room, both men were unpleased at their thoughts as they had no memory of the

night's events only the bruised, battered and leaking bodies told a story, and to these two men, it was not a story that they would like to hear repeated. It would be a long time before these two cocksuckers went to a gay club looking for some action. Meanwhile later that day Tony Ryman rang Jack and told him of the Photographs and video that he had just acquired from the gay party at the hotel. Jack smiled as Tony described some of the night's events. Nothing more than the scum deserve he thought as he put down the phone and turned to Pete to discuss other business.

Chapter Nine

Pete was telling Jack that while they had nothing in particular on at the moment business wise, then maybe it was time to take a trip to South Africa to meet up with the infamous Mr Brown. A week later Jack and Pete stepped off the aeroplane into the warm air at South Africa's Johannesburg airport, they made their way to the baggage carousel to collect their luggage, on collection of their luggage the two men walked through the double doors leading to the arrivals lounge where they were met by the now legendary Mr Ray Brown. Pete did the introductions as the three men walked out of the building towards the car park. It took them just less than half an hour to reach the Hilbrow hotel in the centre of Johannesburg where they would be staying, at least until they had decided either to investigate any of Ray Brown's ideas further or to return home, whichever way it was to turn out, the Hilbrow hotel was only likely to be a temporary accommodation. Two hours after dropping Jack and Pete off at the Hilbrow hotel, Ray returned to the bar to meet up with them once again as they had arranged earlier. Having found a quiet corner to seat themselves, Ray began to repeat some of the stories that he had told to Pete on his previous trip. Jack thought Ray to be quite a convincing storyteller, but wondered how much was fiction to tantalise the listener's ear, and how much was fact and it was only fact that Jack was interested in. Jack was intrigued by Ray's stories of going beyond the seventy-ninth parallel into Namibia; it was South West Africa and a part of South Africa until it was given independence some years ago. It was when he was on his travels in this region when he was working for the South African government that he came upon what the locals call the fields of dreams, it was a large barren area mainly rocks and sand; what made the area interesting was that a lot of the rocks, even the ones at the side of the road contained quality diamonds, Ray went on to say that if you had a geologist with you or just someone that had a bit of knowledge then fortunes could be had for the taking. 'What are the drawbacks?' Jack asked, knowing that there must be some otherwise there would be millions of people up there trawling the land. 'The draw backs, Ray laughed, are the troops, there are signposts everywhere saying do not stop your vehicle and do not pick up any rocks or stones; perpetrators will be shot.' 'I'd say that was a serious drawback Ray.'

'Somewhat old chap, but the idea is to gather as many rocks as possible without being seen.'

'And how do you propose to do that?'
'There are ways but I've not decided which one to try as yet.' 'I think that it needs some serious thought.'
Two days later the three men landed at Windhoek airport, the idea being that they would hire a jeep and while using the pretence of being on a safari expedition, they would use the safari as cover to do some surveillance in the field of dreams area. The following day once the hired jeep was kitted out safari style, the three men headed off to look for the field of dreams. The first area that Ray Brown took them to, was only about sixty kilometres away from Windhoek, but the area couldn't have been more different, it was a timeless, barren looking place on the edge of the Namib desert, Pete mentioned that it looked like pictures he'd seen of the moon, and Jack agreed with him, to the unprepared it would be an unforgiving place, the forty degree burning heat of the day that could turn a man insane followed by the bitterly cold nights that often fell to twenty degrees below freezing, all to often killing the unsuspecting or the ill-equipped. Luckily enough for Jack and Pete their guide had years of survival experience in this environment. They couldn't have been in safer hands. Ray gestured towards the thousands of loose rocks that lay motionless in this burning wasteland.

 'Anyone one of these rocks could be hiding a

fortune.'
'Surely it's like looking for a needle in a haystack?' Jack added.
'Not really, said Ray, there are so many diamond rich rocks out here, the odds are definitely in our favour.'
'It still seems like a lottery.' Pete mumbled.
'No, because if we pick up a bag full of rocks today, and take them back to Windhoek to a guy that I know who deals in these matters, the chances are that some will contain diamonds of some value.'
Jack thought about what Ray was saying, and after a little thought he asked, 'If it's so easy why isn't everyone doing it, and there's another thing that puzzles me and that is if you only have to drive up here and grab a hand full of rocks to make a fortune, then what do you need us for?'
'It's not as easy as it looks, this place is fraught with danger the seen and the unseen but you're right it does look easy to just drive up here, grab a handful of rocks then drive off into the sunset rather rich, but unfortunately it doesn't work like that, first of all you could be completely unlucky and never find anything of value, then even if you do get lucky you then find that the diamond market here is completely fucked up, diamonds have little value compared to the risks so only the few and the foolish are prepared to risk all for very little return, which is where you

come in, because if we find any diamonds of size or quality then the short answer is that they need to be smuggled out of the country and that my friend is an extremely risky business.
'There's always a catch.' Jack iterated. 'Isn't there always?' Pete added.
'You stand to lose nothing by looking and investigating, at the absolute worst scenario, you'll have had an informative holiday and thawed your bones out in the sunshine, on the other hand you might conclude that there's a few rand here and there to be made or in yours case pounds sterling.'
'Did he say a few grand Jack?' asked Pete
'No, I think he meant South African Rand Pete.'
'Oh yeah, right.' Said the thoughtful Pete.
Ray had by now stepped out of the parked vehicle near to a signpost that let them know that they would be shot if found there. He quickly gathered a multitude of rocks and piled them into his bag then swiftly throwing the bag into the vehicle, he fired up the engine and sped away. The three men and their bag of rocks then headed back towards Windhoek, where upon arriving Ray took them to see his friend Jan de Boer, a small tubby white South African who had a room at the rear of a shop on the outskirts of the city, Jan seemed to be a quiet friendly man who obviously had a lot of respect for Ray Brown. Ray left the bag of rocks with Jan de Boer and said that he would

return the following day to see what the results were. The two men shook hands very firmly as they parted company at the door of the shop and after agreeing to meet the following day Ray followed by Jack and Pete returned to the jeep. After catching up on some much needed sleep, and waking the next day refreshed the three men headed off back to Jan de Boers workshop cum office, Ray Brown led the other two men through the front shop into Jan de Boers room at the back of the shop, he had already done the work on the rocks the previous evening after the three men had left, there was nothing substantial in these particular rocks he said, although there were diamond particles, it was nothing to write home about, he wished them better luck next time, the three men turned around to walk out of the shop, when Jack and Pete got to the jeep they noticed that Ray was not with them, it was obvious that for whatever reason, he was still in the shop talking to Jan de Boer. 'I smell a rat Pete.'
'Behave yourself Jack you're just paranoid.'
'Paranoid I might be, but I still smell a rat.'
'This blokes sound Jack, give him a chance?'
'For you Pete I will, but if my heebee jeebees get any worse, I'm on a plane out of here.'
'Okay Jack, but let's give it a chance.'
'Chance is exactly what it is Pete, but I still smell a rat.'
'Ray Brown came out of the shop and jumped

into the jeep, he didn't say a word about why he had stayed behind, and the suspicious Jack took note of this. The three men drove back out to the Namib Desert to gather more stones, each day they drove to a different area, and each day was without success. Every night on their way back to their hotel the men would drop off their bag of rocks with Jan de Boer, and each following day they would get the same answer, a little trace of diamond dust here a little trace there never anything substantial, not even enough to cover the costs of the trip. Back in their shared hotel room Jack told Pete that he thought that they were the victims of some sort of scam, but the only thing that he could think of was that Ray Brown had a deal going with Jan de Boer and the stones they brought back every night weren't just dust traces but real diamonds. 'If that's the case, Pete said, then what does he need us for, he could just drive up there and get the rocks himself?'

'That's a good point Pete.'

'He's hardly likely to hand us a bag of diamonds in a couple of weeks and ask us to smuggle them to Belgium or Israel for him his he?'

'I think that it might arouse our suspicions somewhat Pete.'

'So, give him the benefit of the doubt Jack, at least until he proves otherwise.' 'Well we've come this far a few more days won't harm us.' The conversation changed to thoughts of home and the two men's conversation drifted from the job in hand to the comforts and pleasures of home. The next day out in the Namib desert the plan suddenly changed as Ray decided that while Pete and Jack searched for rocks in one area he would drive to another area, that way they could cover more ground in their search for the prize; Jack was not happy at the idea of being left in a desert in the blazing heat without any form of getaway transport or any shelter from the heat, he was also well aware of the signposts close by saying that they could be shot just for being there, this did not make for a happy chap, each day after that Ray would be gone for longer and longer; Jack complained that they were being burned in the blazing sunshine, but Ray just mumbled that it would be worth it once they'd struck it rich. After a few more days of getting nowhere fast Jack told Pete that he'd had enough and that he was throwing his hand in on the deal, 'To much work with too little reward.' Jack had told him. 'To be honest Jack, I've had enough meself.' Jack and Pete packed their bags and waited for Ray to return before breaking the news to him, 'It's like this Ray, Jack said, we've discussed what's occurring here, and we're not happy.'

'Why what's up?' Ray demanded.

'We're wheeler dealers Ray we duck and dive making the odd shilling here and there, we're not geologists, we're not even manual

workers, this game is not for us.' Ray stood there for a few minutes thinking then He said, 'Listen chaps I've not been altogether honest with you two, I'm in the process of setting up a major diamond robbery.'
'A fuckin robbery, where?' Jack blurted out.
'Everyday when I leave you two in the desert, I've been driving over to a diamond mine to take photographs of it, just to see if it's a feasible project, and I think it is do you fancy coming in on it.'
'Where is this diamond mine?' asked the now interested Jack. 'It's further out in the desert.'
'That figures, what's the security like?'
'The best, it's got everything, from alarms to watch towers, and regular dog patrols.'
'Well that's just helped me to make my mind up, and I'm out of here.'
'Me too.' Spluttered Pete.
'Whoa, slow down a minute, I've got a man on the inside who can sort most of it out for me and he can give me the information on everything else that I need to know.' 'Well inside information is always an advantage, Jack mused, but I'm still not convinced.'
'Jack, Jack, Jack, Ray rambled, before you make up your mind let me show you the photo's and the plan.'
'I'm really not interested. Protested Jack.
'Jack this one hit is worth many millions of pounds.'

'Ah, now I'm interested, show me the plan.'
Ray walked off grinning, to go and get his plan and photographs.' 'I'm not fuckin sure about this Jack.' Pete muttered.

'It'll cost us nothing to see his plans Pete.'
A few minutes later Ray Brown returned to Jack and Pete's room with his hand drawn plan and the photographs, but only the photographs that he wanted the two men to see, he showed the photographs to them and explained his plan in detail, it was as far fetched as a James Bond film, but somehow Ray Brown made it seem possible, and in Jack's mind it was better than fuckin about with old rocks in the desert.

'What do you think then Jack.' Asked the attention-grabbing Mr Brown.

'I'll have to think about it.' Said Jack.

'You'll have to think quick Jack, it's got to be done in eight days time.' 'Why's that?'

'Because if we leave it any longer, this months stock will have been moved, and we don't want to go through all this trouble to rob an empty safe, do we?'

'No, that's for sure.'

'You'll have to let me know by tomorrow or I'll have to make other arrangements.'

'By tomorrow, Jack snapped, that doesn't leave a lot of time.'

'Time is what I don't have a lot of at this stage.' Ray stressed.

'We'll let you know tomorrow Ray.' Jack said as

he handed him his photographs and his plan.'

'Yeah, you do that Jack, and if the answer is yes we'll need another man, can you get one, someone with plenty of bottle?'

'If I'm in, I can always get a good man.' Jack smiled already having an unsuspecting victim in mind. At that point Ray Brown left the room. Pete and Jack spoke for quite some time about the plusses and the pitfalls of getting involved with Ray Brown's plan. They both thrived on adventure but this escapade seemed a bit too much for Pete's nerves, it was one of those times when his sixth sense was screaming at him to pack his bags and go home, the problem that Pete felt that he had was Jack's lack of foresight in the face of imminent danger, he felt that at times Jack took some unnecessary risks, with Pete's life as well as his own. It was the next morning that Jack asked Pete about what his thoughts were on doing the job with Ray Brown. Pete said that he wasn't keen on it but he would go with whatever Jack was going to do, Pete's inner feeling of impending doom told him that Jack was going to take this adventure by the horns, and he wasn't wrong. 'I'm going to give it a shot, Jack said calmly, we've come this far, another week and we'll be out of here and hopefully with some diamonds.'

'If you're in, I'm in.' Pete gulped nervously. Before Ray Brown arrived at their room Jack left to make some phone calls. The first number he

tried several times but got no response, eventually giving up on the number, he rang his brother Charles. 'Charles it's me Jack.'
'Where the fuck are you? Charles demanded, no-ones heard off you or seen you for ages, Sandra's going off her head.'
'Right, right, tell her I'm okay and I'll be back in a week or two.' 'Okay but she won't be happy.'
'She will be when I get home.'
'Next you're going to tell me that you've got a problem.' Jack laughed and said, 'Only a small one.'
'And what's that.'
'I've been trying to ring a mate of mine in Truro, but his phone isn't responding, if I give you his number can you try it from over there? If you get through tell him I'm trying to get hold of him.'
'Yeah, no problem.'
Jack gave Charlie Smith's number to Charles and left him to sort it out, telling him that he'd ring him back in a couple of hours. Meanwhile back at Jack's hotel room the infamous Mr Ray Brown had returned to see what the answer would be from the two men. 'I don't know what's happening yet, Pete said, you'll have to wait until Jack gets back.' Just at that moment Jack walked in through the door. 'Good morning Jack.' Said the wide-awake Ray Brown. 'And good morning to you Mr Brown.' Jack smiled. 'Do you ever tell Pete anything?

He never seems to know anything about anything.' 'That's our Pete, Jack grinned, the last of the silent men.' 'That may be all well and good, but I was just wondering what your position is, on the matters that we discussed yesterday.'

'We've thought about it, and we've come a long way thus far, so we're in.' 'I was afraid that you were going to say that Jack.' Pete butted in. 'Well it's pointless going home empty handed after all that fuckin diggin around for useless rocks.'

'I suppose you're right.' Said the worried Pete. 'We just need one more man for the Job Jack, can you get someone?' 'I'm working on it; I've got someone in mind.'

'Pointless going back out looking for rocks then, you might as well get a few days rest while I get the necessary equipment organised, ... can you definitely get an extra man?' 'I'll sort it out, you just get your part organised, we'll go over the plan again in a few days when you get back.

'A couple of hours later Jack rang Charles back, 'Did you have any luck with Charlie Smith's phone number.'

'No mate, I think it must be cut off, ...is it urgent?'

'Very.'

'Is there anything else we can do?'

'Yeah, we could send someone to his house.'

'Who?'
'Can't you think of someone?'
'Not off the top of my head.'
'Nor me, I'll get back to ya if I think of someone, in the meantime if you find someone, send them down to Cornwall to his house, and tell them to buy a mobile phone for him en route so that I can speak to him.'
'Okay, you best give me his address, just in case.'
'Yeah, it'd be handy, he lives at Trelander east in Truro, see if you can track him down, I'll ring you tomorrow to see how you've got on.'
The two men put down their phones and went about their business, Charles to see if he could find someone to take a mobile phone down to Cornwall, and Jack to the hotel's swimming pool for some relaxation and to soothe his skin that was burnt in the desert's heat while he was searching for diamonds amongst a sea of rocks. Ray Brown wasn't seen again that day. The following afternoon Jack rang Charles to see if he'd had any results on finding someone to drive down to Charlie's with a mobile phone. 'I'm glad that you've rang Jack, said Charles, I've got a man down in Cornwall as we speak, and there's no answer at that address.'
'Who've ya sent?'
'Kev Croughts gone down with his Mrs Mel.'
Jack laughed, Kev probably won't come back

for a week.'
'You might be right, what should I tell him when he rings me back?'
'Tell him to find Bunters bar in the centre of Truro, tell him to look for the biggest bastard in there, and if he's got a skull tattooed on one side of his neck and a cannabis leaf on the other side, then chances are he's found Charlie.'
'What happens if someone else matches that description?' Charles laughed.
'Fuck off you mad head, there's not two on the planet that look like that, never mind in a tiny dot like Truro.' Jack smiled to himself thinking, two like Charlie Smith, I don't think so. Later that day when Jack rang Charles; Charles gave Jack the telephone number to the mobile phone that Kev Croughton had now delivered to the notorious and elusive Charlie Smith. A few minutes later Jack had rung the mobile number and got through to Charlie Smith. 'You're a hard man to find Charlie.'
'And I'm keeping it that way.' He laughed.
'Yeah Charlie, you never know who's looking.'
Charlie laughed and said, 'That's just what I mean.'
'Anyway Charlie there's a bit of work if you're interested.'
'I'm always interested in a bit of good quality work, do you want me to come over to your house and see you?'
'Charlie I'm in the middle of fuckin Africa.'

'Africa Jack, what the fuck are you doing there? On second thoughts don't answer that.'
'I wasn't going to, if you're interested I'll get Charles to telex some money down to you tomorrow, have you got a current passport?'
'Yeah.'
'Right here's the plan...' Jack went on to explain to Charlie that he'd have to get a flight to Johannesburg first, before re-organising at Johannesburg airport and taking a flight to Windhoek, which is the capital of Namibia. He gave Charlie the phone number of the hotel and his room number so that Charlie could ring him once he got to Windhoek from there Jack would collect him and only then would he let him know what was going on. Charlie Smith thought that it was a big risk, but on the other hand he wasn't really doing anything else at that moment and he was reasonably sure that Jack wouldn't draw him into anything that was to life threatening. Three days later there was still no sign of Charlie Smith, or Ray Brown. Jack and Pete just hung around the hotel mixing with other tourists trying not to attract any attention to themselves. Early the next day Jack was awoken from his bed by the ringing phones continuous annoyance, he wobbled across the floor with half open eyes, until he found the menacing machine.' Only the sound of Charlie Smith's voice saying that he was at the airport accelerated Jack from the living dead zombie

struggling to find the phone to the wide-awake and alert creature that he normally was. 'Stay where you are, he shouted I'll be straight there to get you.' 'Okay, okay, just make it quick coz I'm knackered. Charlie answered. A short while later Jack turned up at the airport to collect Charlie in a hire car that he'd borrowed off one of the other hotel guest's, the two men greeted each other with laughter and a strong shaking of hands. 'It don't look a bad place this Namibia.' Said Charlie 'It's a wasteland outside the city Charlie.' Jack stated as he started the car and drove away. Charlie picked a piece of ripped paper up out of the footwell and read it. The heading was just one word Namibia, Charlie continued to read the rest of the page it read, Namibia is a dry land, largely taken up by a dusty plain dotted with trees and covered with sparse pasture for cattle, sheep and goats. Along the coast of the Atlantic Ocean are the sandy wastes of the Namib Desert, one of the driest places on Earth. In the east, spreading into Botswana is another arid wilderness, the Kalahari Desert. Droughts are common and Namibian farmers must struggle to grow crops of maize and millet in this harsh landscape. However, the terrain does conceal Namibia's natural wealth - it's reserves of dia. Charlie looked into the footwell for the other piece of the torn paper, but it wasn't there. 'Bastard.' He mumbled.

'What was that Charlie?' Jack asked.
'Oh nothing mate, just taking in the scenery.' was his reply. 'Not bad scenery Charlie but it gets worse.'
'What's the job Jack?' asked Charlie thoughtfully.
'I wondered how long it would take you to get to that, actually Charlie it's a diamond robbery.'
'Diamonds eh!' Charlie muttered.
'It's a large diamond mine actually out in the desert, apparently a friend of ours has got inside information about what's in the safe in there at certain times and from what I'm told there's quite a stock in there right now.'
'How long before we hit it?' Charlie enquired.
'A couple of days.'
'Have you seen it?'
'No, I've seen photographs though.'
'Photographs!'
'Yeah photographs and a plan, it's a bit difficult to get near the place.'
'Oh fuckin magic, this is starting to sound extremely fuckin dodgy.'
'Nothings ever easy Charlie especially when we're talking millions of pounds.' Charlie coughed and cleared his throat, 'Millions of pounds eh, well that throws a different light on it, it's got to be worth at least a little look.' Jack and Charlie arrived back at the hotel and on entering Jack's room Jack said, 'Where the fuck have you been?' to the elusive Ray Brown, who

was laying back in a chair swigging from a can of beer.' Ray Brown tried to sit up quickly and finished up coughing and spluttering as he nearly choked on the mouthful of alcohol that he had just tipped into his mouth. 'I told you that drinking was bad for you Ray.' 'Funny Bastard.' He spluttered. The other men in the room looked on smiling at the amusing situation. 'This is Charlie, Jack said, introducing him to Ray, and Charlie the guy choking to death is Ray. Charlie walked over to where Ray was sat and held out his hand, Ray leaned forward and taking Charlie's hand in his own they shook hands briefly. Charlie turned to Pete and shook hands with him also, now with all the introductions over, Ray put the photographs of the mine onto the table for all to see, he then put his hand drawn plan onto the floor so that they could all discuss the parts they had to play looking and pointing at the photographs Charlie said, 'they wouldn't happen to be machine gun towers by any chance would they?'

Charlie unconvincingly laughed and said that they were just look out posts. 'Look like machine gun posts to me.' Charlie mumbled. When Ray had given his orders on who was to do what and where, the men all offered opinions before eventually all agreeing on an exact plan. Jack thought this to be very much like a military operation, there was going to be explosives set off to divert the security, gunshots to confuse all and sundry in the dark, a lot of sneaking about to find the diamonds then out of there quickly, sounds easy when you say it quick Jack thought, and not forgetting in all the confusion the way back to where the escape vehicle would be hidden. 'So everyone's agreed.' Said Ray 'Just one question then Ray, Jack asked, When we doing it?' 'Tomorrow night boys.' 'Tomorrow.' The other three blurted out practically in unison.

'Yep, tomorrows the night, and everything's ready, we've got all the gear the weapons and the extra man, so why wait any longer?' 'Tomorrow night's the night then.' Jack acknowledged. The other men just looked at him and nodded their heads in agreement. 'Best get some rest, for the rest of today, take it easy nothing physical, stay out of the pool, and it's a must that we all get as much sleep as possible tomorrow daytime, tomorrow night we need to be wide awake. Ray left the other three men and agreed to return to collect them the following evening. Jack, Pete and Charlie sat around chatting for a while before going out into the night's warm air to find something to eat. Later on their return, their minds buzzing about the following nights work, they sat around for hours discussing the ins and outs of the whole project, it came to light that none of them liked the idea to much, but the payday looked like being a good one, and at the end of the day they were only in the business that they were in for the money. In the game of chance it's nearly always the bigger the risk the bigger the payday. It helped that they stayed up chatting for most of the night, it made it easier for them to sleep for most of the day and even when Jack and Pete arose around teatime the jet lagged Charlie was still comatose. It was around seven o'clock when Ray arrived, Charlie had eventually risen and was now drowning himself in the shower, strange noises came from the shower room, but no one ventured to see what was going on. When the shower door eventually opened Charlie wandered out drying his hair and singing Eric Claptons `Wonderful Tonight' the notes were going up and down as his head twisted to the throes of the towel rubbing his head. 'You lot ready then?' The three men all dressed in dark clothing nodded in his direction. This was going to be a night to remember, a thought that passed through all their minds for one reason or another. Ray took his time driving the one hundred kilometres to the spot he had chosen to conceal their vehicle; it was as close to the mine has he had dared to go without blatantly attracting the attention of the perimeter guards. The four men all aware of their individual tasks stepped out of the vehicle and one at a time, they took from Ray a haversack containing a small amount of equipment that

each of them would need, each of the men checked the contents of their haversack before re-fastening it and slipping it over their shoulders. Ray then passed each of the men a rifle and a box of ammunition, 'What the fuck do we need these for?' Jack asked.
'Just for confusion purposes.' Ray lied.
'Confused me already.' Charlie added.
Once the men were ready, they trekked the two hundred and odd metres to a ridge overlooking the fairly well lit mining camp, they were still three hundred metres from the perimeter fence, The plan was that they would all meet back at this same spot on the ridge after the robbery before heading for the vehicle, the four men synchronised their watches before Pete and Charlie set off to create havoc on the far side of the mine. Ray and Jack crept as close as they could to the perimeter fence without being noticed. Ray took some wire cutters from a pocket on his large rucksack; the two men then lay still and waited. It was half an hour later when the first explosion destroyed the tranquility of the night followed swiftly by the sky being illuminated, the sound of a siren blaring also cut through the nights stillness, Jack and Ray still unmoving near to the perimeter fence could hear the sound of footsteps, they continued to remain motionless a little longer, once the sound of footsteps dwindled into the distance, Ray bobbed his

head up and took a look around, another explosion in the distance once again broke the silence, Ray moved towards the perimeter fence and quickly began to cut through it with his cutters, once he had cut a big enough slit into the fence, he motioned to Jack to follow him and on doing so he slipped through the fence into the compound quickly followed by Jack. They made their way around the cabin type buildings, trying to avoid being spotted by the guards in the watchtowers. The guards hopefully were otherwise engaged in Pete and Charlie's firework display. It wasn't long before Ray had got to the building that he wanted to enter, he got in but the alarm went off, Jack remained outside to watch out for guards and although the alarm sounded very loud to Jack, it was mostly drowned out by the screaming siren blaring out around the camp. It was ten minutes before Ray resurfaced from the building though to Jack it felt like hours. The men headed back to the fence and then into the ditch where they had lay earlier, they could hear people running and shouting all around them but the screaming siren made it difficult to pinpoint the exact location of the other noises. Ray looked at his watch, and then whispered to Jack that they were running late, at that same moment another much louder explosion ripped through the night, Jack and Ray used this as cover to make their escape.

When they got back to the ridge Charlie and Pete were already there waiting for them. The noise of a couple of jeeps approaching caused the four men to take cover, once the jeep had passed, Ray suggested a small change of plan, he would go and get the jeep while the other men took cover, 'It's easier for one of us to stay out of sight than all of us.' The other three men nodded in agreement, but the suspicious Jack added, 'No point in taking your rucksack with you Ray if you're bringing the vehicle to us.' Ray looked at Jack and smirked. 'Not very trusting are you Jack?' Ray said has he handed his rucksack to Jack. Jack just looked on, saying nothing. As Ray slipped away into the darkness to fetch the vehicle, Pete said, 'Fuckinell Jack, that was a bit over the top.' Jack's reply was, 'The only way out of here is in that fuckin jeep, if he doesn't come back we're fucked, if he's got a bag full of diamonds and the jeep, he might not fancy coming back to split it four ways.'

'I never thought of that Jack.' Pete whispered. 'Well I did, there's something not quite right with our Mr Brown.' 'And what's that?'

'I don't know, I can't quite put my finger on it.' Another jeep passed close by, and the three men took cover, Jack however raised his head enough to see that there were four men in the vehicle and at least two of them were carrying rifles. Ray by now had reached the jeep; his idea was that his jeep would blend in with the other jeeps that were flying around for long enough for him and his men to make their getaway. As Ray headed the couple of hundred metres back to collect his men another jeep approached, then without any warning the guards opened fire on Ray, and without hesitation Ray fired back. The two vehicles got within yards of each other, still firing wildly in the darkness, in all the commotion Ray didn't realise that one of the guards had tossed a grenade into his vehicle it was only seconds later that the device exploded sending the legendary Ray Brown to his death and destroying the other three men's only means of escape in the process. The three men watched the series of events the best they could from their position, they couldn't see exactly what had gone on, they only caught glimpses of movements in the darkness, they could hear the sound of gunfire, and they heard the sound of the grenade exploding but they didn't know what it was, Jack motioned for the other two men to follow him as he sneaked nearer to the smoldering wreck some two hundred yards away. The three men took cover as two other jeeps appeared, their blazing lights cutting through the night's darkness, and the two jeeps skidded to a halt as they approached the mangled wreck, a number of men got out of the jeeps and circled what was left of the vehicle, after a few minutes one of the jeeps sped away leaving two men to guard the lump of twisted metal. Jack whispered to the others, 'There's something wrong here, these are not normal guards, they're soldiers tooled up to the fucking eyeballs, we don't know where Ray is, so we're going to have to make our own way out of here, and we'll have to do it quickly before the others get back.'

'Do you know the way Jack?' Pete whispered.
'Not a clue.' Jack said shrugging his shoulders.
'Fuckinell, Pete mumbled as the blood ran from his now pale face.

The three men crept to within thirty yards of the two soldiers, the soldiers stood around casually smoking waiting for reinforcements to arrive, neither of them heard nor felt the bullets that felled them, the smoking barrels of Jack and Charlie's rifles would remain embedded on Pete's mind forever, he was in shock. Charlie scrambled from where they had been lay and ran towards the jeep, Pete who was still in shock had to be dragged along by Jack for a few seconds until he snapped out of his trance like state, the three men boarded the jeep, Jack took the driving position and spun the vehicle around, he flicked the headlights on momentarily to get some bearings as to where the track was, and has he did the battered and bloodied remains of Ray Brown came into view, Pete almost threw up at the sight. Jack

flicked the headlights off and drove as swiftly as he could in the darkness without lights, once they had travelled more than a mile from the scene, Jack asked Charlie to lean over the back of the jeep and smash the rear lights which he did with the butt of his rifle, it was then that Jack turned the headlights back on to assist in their getaway. Jack could recognise no landmarks in the darkness, he was just living in hope that he was going the right way, 'How do you know that you're going the right way Jack?' asked the now terrified Pete.
'I don't, said Jack, but if that's the North Star up there, and I'm hoping that it is, then we're roughly going in the right direction.'
'North Star, roughly.' Pete stammered.
Charlie sat in the back quietly bemused by the night's events but keeping his eyes open for anything unusual that might add to their nights adventure. Luckily for the three men they were back on civilised roads before the jeep that they had `borrowed' ran out of fuel, daylight had broken through and now the three men were visible and by that fact they were now vulnerable. They marched for nearly an hour before a convoy of four vehicles returning from a safari stopped to pick them up. Jack explained to his new hosts that they'd had a puncture and had to leave their vehicle behind. They sped on towards Windhoek. About five miles further along the road they came across

an army roadblock, as the four vehicles slowed down the three men looked at each other in disbelief. The soldiers asked the drivers of the vehicles where they had been, they also asked them for papers which the drivers produced, while this was going on other soldiers were searching the vehicles, checking some of the bags and rooting through the safari peoples equipment. After a few minutes they were waved on to continue their journey, the relief on Jack and Charlie's faces was noticeable, Pete however was in urgent need of a toilet, he didn't think that his bowels would last the rest of the journey to Windhoek. On arriving at Windhoek the three men thanked their hosts for their help and wished them a safe trip home. One of the drivers winked to Jack and said that he thought they were very lucky at the roadblock. Jack smiled, said nothing but showing his gratitude he shook the man's hand. All three men went back to the hotel and collected their belongings, they moved to another less attention-attracting place on the outskirts of the city. This was the first opportunity that the men had to look at the stash of diamonds in Rays bag. Jack opened the bag and found two quite large strange looking flasks; he stopped Charlie from opening one.
'We don't know what's in there Charlie.'
'Hopefully it's diamonds Jack.'
 'What if it's not?'

'Well let's have a look?'
'I smell a rat here, let's go and see Ray's mate before we open anything.'
The three men arrived at Jan de Boer's place of work, Pete stayed in the vehicle while Jack and Charlie went in.'
'Hello, said Jan de Boer, where's Ray?'
'I'd like to talk to you about Ray, what was the job he was doing?'
'That's between me and Ray.'
'Not any more it's not.'
'Why's that?'
'Because Ray's no longer in the land of the living.'
Jan de Boer ranted and raved in some language that Jack did not understand. 'Hey speak English.' Jack shouted to the irate man.
'Okay, what happened to him?'
'Tell me first about the job.'
'The job was that he was going to rob a mine out in the desert.'
'Sounds simple enough.'
'No, it's not, it's very heavily guarded.'
'I thought it might be.'
'So what's happened to Ray?'
'Oh, he's been blown up, I think possibly by a grenade.'
Jan de Boer started ranting and raving again in some sort of panic attack. Jack slapped him in the face and asked him what was up. Jan de Boer explained that the goods that Ray was

going to rob were going to be passed on to some contacts of de Boers from the Middle East. 'Well just tell them that the deal is off.'
'In that I've got no choice, but they've already laid out a lot of money.' 'Money, what for?'
'Expenses, and I had to pay Ray up front.'
'Whoa, slow down because you've lost me here, what exactly was Ray getting for you.'
'Don't you know?'
'No, but I'm getting impatient.'
'He went to the mine, working off inside information that I'd given him to steal two flasks.'
'Well that explains the flasks, what's in the fuckin flasks.'
'Oh our Mr Brown has really taken you for a ride.'
'What was in the fuckin flasks?' Jack demanded.
'The flasks my friend contain uranium 235.'
'235, that means that its been processed.'
'That's right my friend capable of making a nuclear bomb.'
'What the fuck as this got to do with a diamond mine?'
Jan de Boer started to laugh, 'He's really had you over, diamond mine, there's no diamond mine, it's a uranium mine and below ground unbeknown to the world it has its own processing plant.'
'Fucking hell.' Charlie wheezed.
'That's an understatement Charlie.' Jack added.
'Where's the flasks now?' asked de Boer.

'What does it matter?'
'It matters to me, I've already paid Ray, and the Iraqis will be on my case.' 'Why did you pay him up front?'
'He said that he had to pay his men up front, I should have twigged when he wanted paying in diamonds.'
'You paid him in diamonds.'
'Yes, why?'
'Nothing, I was just thinking aloud.'
'Where are the flasks now?' De Boer pleaded.
'I'm not sure, maybe I can find them for a fee.'
'Yes, yes, I will pay you well if you can get the flasks for me.'
'I'll get back to you.' Jack said as he left with Charlie.
The two men got into the car with Pete.
'Anything out of the ordinary Pete?' Jack asked.
'Not that I've noticed.'
Jack pulled up outside the hotel that they had left earlier that day, he told Pete to wait in the car and keep his eye out for anything unusual. Jack and Charlie slipped into the hotel by the rear stairway so as not to be noticed, they tried to force the door of Ray's room but without success, just when they were about to leave; the door of the next apartment opened and a young couple stepped out about to leave, when Jack butted into their conversation, explaining that he was from the next apartment but couldn't get in because he'd mislaid his keys, he asked them

if he could go through their apartment onto the balcony while he climbed onto his own balcony, he explained that he had a spare set of keys inside. The holiday couple were a bit apprehensive at first but the young man allowed himself to be convinced by Jack. He let the two men into the apartment, he opened the patio doors onto his balcony, and before he could get any words out of his mouth Jack had gone over the balcony fencing and leapt onto the adjoining apartment's balcony. The young man locked his balcony door and followed Pete onto the walkway outside, as the young man locked his door the door opened of the next apartment and Jack bobbed his head out. 'Thanks very much.' Jack shouted. 'It was nothing.' The man shouted as he walked off.

Jack pulled the door open wider and Charlie entered the room. 'What are we looking for Jack?' Charlie enquired.

'Anything of value, especially diamonds.'

'I'm on it.' Charlie said as he went about his business.

The two men searched the apartment for quite some time finding only a few hundred South African Rand and some American dollars. A while later Charlie found a small safe hidden in the bedroom; he struggled for a while to open it whilst Jack looked on in some amusement. When Charlie did eventually open the steel box, it contained nothing of value, only some false passports and some personal affects belonging to Ray.

Jack suggested that they tidy the place up before they left in case anyone came along and thought it a might suspicious, Charlie had overturned a draw onto the floor to mooch through it, once he had put all the big pieces back into the draw there was still a lot of crumbs covering the floor, Jack told him to hoover it up while he took the panel off the side of the bath. A few minutes later when Jack returned looking for a screwdriver he noticed that the hoover cable was stretched across the apartment. 'What the fuck are you doing Charlie?' Jack asked.

'What do you mean?'

'Why've ya stretched the cable, there's a socket near the door.'

'It doesn't work.' Charlie shouted back.

'Typical of foreign electrics.' Jack mumbled as he picked up a knife to use as a screwdriver. Jack went back to the bathroom and proceeded to take the side off the bath, there was nothing behind it other than the pipes that were supposed to be there. Jack replaced the panel and returned the knife to the kitchen. He then stood around watching Charlie clear up the mess that he'd made while ransacking the place. It was only while Jack was stood about mindlessly thinking that the cable flapping about across the room in front of him gave him an idea. Jack took a table lamp across the room and plugged it into both of the plugholes in the double socket first one then the other both times there was no response, Jack shook his head in wonder then went to find a small screwdriver, there wasn't one, he had to make do with a long thin bladed knife which he forced into the narrow holes that led to the screws, once the screws were undone the double socket which was a false front for a little wall safe came off. He had no keys to undo the safe so he gave Charlie the task of retrieving the small metal box. Charlie had a swift method of retrieval; he just went into the next room and prodded about until he was in the right area, then he sat on the floor and stamped his booted foot into the wall causing the metal box to eject from the other side, there was quite some damage. The two men were just about halfway through cleaning up when there was a loud banging on the door. Jack went to look, he looked through the spy-hole in the door and didn't like what he saw, and he ran back to the main room and shouted to Charlie, 'It's the fuckin odd-lot.' 'Bollox.' 'Follow me,' he said as he headed for the patio doors.

Charlie followed him and together they managed to lock the patio doors behind them, Jack climbed the fence on the balcony and jumped to the balcony of the apartment next door. 'Throw the box to me Charlie.' He shouted.

Charlie threw the box, which Jack caught and put on the floor. 'Come on Charlie jump.' Jack shouted.
'It's a long way down.'
'You're not jumping down, are you?'
'You're right Jack.' He laughed as he jumped from one balcony to the other.
Jack helped Charlie to get over the barrier on the balcony, then the two men opened the patio door and went inside, Charlie wanted to leave but Jack convinced him to stay put, Charlie sat down and Jack put the kettle on, it was Jack's cushion in times of crisis a good cup of tea. It wasn't long before the two quiet men could hear noises and voices coming from the next apartment. They were stranded for the next one and a half hours before it was safe to leave. Before leaving Jack left the South African Rand and American dollars that he'd found earlier on the table of the young couples apartment as a way of saying thanks for their hospitality. Eventually they got back to the car. 'Where the fuck have you two been, I've been burning to death in here.' Pete ranted. 'Let's get away from here chaps.' Jack declared.
'I need a drink.' Pete stated.
'I've just had one.' Charlie said.
Pete glared at the two men and said nothing, after a short drive Jack parked outside a cafe, the three men went in and ordered a meal and

some drinks. Pete was very thirsty. After leaving the cafe Jack called at a hardware shop and bought some tools, they then drove to an out of the way place where they could make some noise and demolition Charlie smashed open the steel safe, inside the safe were four bags of diamonds, one for each of the men.

'Why were we risking our lives and liberty if the diamonds were already at Ray's apartment?' Charlie asked.

This is my theory, said Jack, and with Ray gone it can only ever be a theory. We weren't ever supposed to find out that the mine was anything other than a diamond mine, therefore if we'd have all got back, then Ray would have gone off with his bag returning the next day with a little bag of diamonds each for us, and then he'd have rode off into the sunset with a couple of flasks of uranium 235 worth absolute fortunes in the Middle East. 'Now we've got both we'll be double rich.' Said Pete grinning. 'No we won't.' Jack replied.

'What do you mean?' asked the surprised Pete.

'I mean the Iraqi's aren't getting it off us.'

'Who then?'

'We'll give it back.'

'Give.'

'Yeah, give, if we try to do any deals, we'll get nicked.'

'Fuck to getting nicked Jack.' Charlie added.

'So lets not be greedy and settle for what we've

got, agreed.'
'Agreed.' said Pete.
'Agreed.' said Charlie.
Two days later just before their flight left Windhoek for the U.K., Jack telephoned the local newspaper to tell them where they could find the two lead lined flasks that contained the deadly product of uranium 235. The three men should now have been relaxed heading for home and leaving their troubles behind them, but for now they had a more imminent problem, and that was that all three men had swallowed packages containing diamonds, neither of them had eaten for the past two days and now even on this long trip home they could only drink water. When the other passengers ate their food the three men could only look on in agony and lick their lips. They were already in mid flight when the police raided Ray's apartment for the second time, this time in the middle of the room in full view of all who entered were the two lead lined flasks. Jack was sat thinking and trying to put all the pieces together, he concluded that he would never know what the whole truth was and now as he headed home did it really matter, the only losers were the guards at the uranium mine for they had lost their lives, the only financial losers were Jan de Boer and his Middle Eastern friends. Jack had no time to worry about them. He drifted to sleep, only to be woken sometime later when

someone complained about his snoring. There was some relief on the men's faces when the Captain announced that they would soon be landing at Heathrow airport. Pete leaned across Jack so that he could look out of the window as the plane came down. It seemed like a long time from when the plane landed until they finally disembarked. Then there was another long wait while the luggage came through on the carousel, the men had previously agreed to split up at the carousel and walk through the customs area singly so as not to attract to much attention to themselves. The packages of diamonds had all been interned for to long by now and were waiting to be ejected from the three men's bodies at the nearest toilet. Jack went through first and was immediately arrested on production of his passport. The other two men on seeing Jack being carted off by the odd-lot had visions of impending doom. All this work for nothing Charlie thought to himself. Fifteen minutes later Charlie and Pete met up outside the airport at their prearranged place. 'What the fuck was all that about?' Charlie asked.
'Not a clue, said Pete, we'll have to wait and see.'
'What can we do?' Charlie asked.
'The best thing for you to do for now is to fuck off back to Cornwall, and as for me once I get home and plot my diamonds up, I'll go and see Jack's Mrs, and find out what's going on.' The

following day Jack was transferred to his local police station where he was quizzed about the disappearance of Slippery Sam Edwards. Jack refused to speak until his solicitor got there and it would be another day before Mr Giovanni Di Stefano arrived from his office in Rome. It was only when Jack's solicitor had arrived and spoken with the police that it was brought to Jack's attention that they had found a body that they believed was that of the missing Sam Edwards, and that they had heard through the grapevine that Jack and Sam were rivals who had, had several run ins over the years. Jack refused to answer any questions and after several words to the police from Mr Di Stefano, Jack was given police bail. Jack walked out of the police station and into the arms of Sandra who he had not seen for quite some time. Jack thanked Mr Di Stefano as Mr Di Stefano rushed to his waiting car in the hope that he could catch his return flight to Rome. Jack collapsed into the passenger seat of his car and said, 'I'm knackered San, take me home.'
'You bet.' She smiled.
'It's been a long fucking year.' Jack mumbled to himself.

Chapter Ten

On realising that Jack was no longer in custody, Pete rushed round to Jack's house to find out what was going on. Jack freshly showered having not long forced himself out of bed and still in his dressing gown sat down at the kitchen table with Pete. Sandra poured the tea, while Jack explained that the odd-lot had found a body that they thought was slippery Sam's and with all the grief between the two men over recent times, Jack had become a suspect in his demise. Another problem that Jack had had for the last few days was the diamonds, he explained to Pete that he'd had to get them out when he was arrested at the airport, he'd gone to the toilet and got them out then he'd had to wash the packages and force them back in again, he'd then been moved to a different police station hundreds of miles away and over the next couple of days he'd had to repeat the process many times until Giovanni had got him out on bail. He told Pete that he was extremely relieved that he had now got the diamonds out of his body for the last time. 'If only the odd-lot had realised that I was sat on a fortune.' Jack laughed. 'Where there's muck

there's money.' Pete sniggered.
Jack said that he'd had enough of globetrotting, risking life and limb in the hope of earning a shilling or two. 'Best if we stay close to home Pete and earn a crust the way we know best.'
'I think it's time to retire Jack.'
'Depends what we get for the diamonds.'
'That's a point.'
'Well I'm sure that you don't want to retire skint.'
'No, you're right but the last couple weeks have aged me so much, I might be able to get a pension.'
'I know the feeling, I'm to old for all this wing and a prayer bollocks.'
'There's no money in the pot game, and we don't do class A's, we could still squeeze a few quid out of the cigs, but it's not regular.'
'I'll have a think Pete, maybe there's something else, that I can come up with.'
'Well if you do, make sure that it's safer than the last idea.' Pete grinned.'
'Hey bollocks, that fuckin Ray Brown job is down to you.'
'That makes a change.'
'I won't be fuckin listening to you again, that's for sure; you and he's a nice bloke. We should know better, because if something looks to good to be true it usually is.'
'In our case it always is.' Pete said as he got up to

leave.
'I'll meet up with you tomorrow Pete.'
'Where?'
'We'll have a change of venue, how does
the Jolly Falstaff sound at two o'clock.'
'Sounds good to me.'
'Don't tell a soul, we don't want anymore
unexpected incidents.'
'You're right there Jack, til tomorrow then'
Pete said as he left the house closing the
door behind him.'
The following afternoon around four thirty, Jack
left the table where he'd been sat in the Jolly
Falstaff and headed out onto the car park.
Unbeknown to Jack he was being watched from
the side of two steel shipping containers that had
been left on the far side of the car park for so long
that they had blended into the scenery. Jack was
almost at his car when the two, baseball bat
wielding men made their appearance. Jack not
wishing to be bashed around the head by one of
these lunatics ran around the cars on the car park
to avoid being hit by the bats, within seconds Pete
and other men who had spotted the incident
through the pub window ran out of the pub
carrying bottles and glasses with them as
weapons, the two would be attackers fled from
the car park and escaped onto a housing estate in
the hope of making a clean getaway away. Jack
had other plans; he asked a couple of the guys
from the pub to follow the thugs on foot while he

and three others drove around a different way and scoured the estate, Jack saw one of the men getting into a car, his accomplice was at least one hundred yards behind him, Jack raced towards the car, but as he did so the attacker who was in the car raced off leaving his confused and disorientated associate behind, the already breathless man tried to run, but his lung capacity had expired he was carried a few more yards on adrenalin before being lifted of his weary feet and dumped into the boot of Jack's car. Jack went back to the Jolly Falstaff car park and dropped off two of the men who had helped him to hunt down his attacker. As he drove off the car park 'A job for B.T. Pete.' Jack smiled.
'Oh shit, Pete drawled, that sounds fuckin painful.'
'Let's hope so.' Jack said as he drove away to look for a phone box.
A few hours later B.T. returned Jack's car minus the body that had been in the boot earlier.
'Did he have much to say feller?' Jack asked.
'A bit, but nothing I could make total sense of.'
'Go on then let's hear it.'
'Right, first of all him and his mate have been sent by a mob from Liverpool called the Gardeners.'
'Never heard of them.'
'Well some guy called Frenchie went missing, and after much investigation they've put it down to you.'

'Didn't know that the dirty thieving bastard had any friends.'
'He's not.'
'What is that supposed to mean?'
'Gardners sister, Gaynor went to Spain to join Frenchie, and she's never been seen since.'
'Fucking hell.'
'Have you done her in Jack?'
'Have I fuck, I've never heard of her before today.'
'Well they think you've done their sister in and that's why you've been getting attacked left, right and centre.'
'Where've they been getting their information from, as to my whereabouts?' 'Some doorman from a nightclub near to you, he didn't know his name.' 'A fucking doorman, that doesn't make any sense, he must be lying.' 'Maybe, but he was definitely terrified when he told me.' 'Where is he now?'
'Fuck knows, I threw him out on the Motorway.'
'How fast was you going at the time?'
B.T. just grinned and Jack was left without an answer.
Jack drove B.T. back to where he'd left his car earlier, when he'd taken Jack's vehicle with the attacker in the boot.
Jack then met up with Pete, and asked him to check around about the local doorman who had access to more than enough information about

Jack's movements. Just then Jack's phone rang it was Charlie 'Awright Jack what we doing with these fuckin stones, can't fuckin spend'em darn here.' Charlie said in his best Cornish mockney accent.
'Head over this way in a day or two and I'll get them sorted for ya.' 'Will do Jack.'
'Did you hear what happened to me?'
'Yeah, I spoke to Pete the other day, we'll talk some more when I get down to your end.'
'That'll be better.'
'See you soon.' Charlie shouted as he cut the line dead before getting a reply.
Armed with new information Jack set about investigating the Gardner family. Charlie made an appearance the following day, with only a small package of diamonds for his luggage. A little later in the day Jack took the diamonds from Charlie and gave them to another man who inspected them, then after nodding his head several times he proceeded to leave the room. Charlie jumped up quickly and grabbed the man around the neck, 'Where ya going with my fuckin diamonds.' He shouted. The choking man couldn't answer. Jack on pulling the two men apart said to Charlie it's okay the guy's not going anywhere.' Charlie half apologised and sat down. The other man left the room with the diamonds. Jack said 'Fuckin ell Charlie I thought you were gonna kill the poor bastard.'
'I was, after all I've been through to get the

bastard things, no-ones gonna just walk off with them, while I sit around like a plum.'

'Yeah, I can see that.' Jack grinned.

The man returned a few minutes later and gave Charlie a large brown envelope full of money, Charlie opened it up and looked inside, 'What the fuck's this?' He declared handing the package to Jack, Jack looked inside and said it's okay Charlie they're only euros.'

'euros fuckin euros, what am I supposed to do with them in Bunters fuckin bar?'

'Don't worry Charlie, I'll change them for you.'

'Cheers Jack, you're a pal.

'Hmmm.' Jack mumbled.

Jack's phone rang and he walked away from the two men whispering into the mouthpiece of his mobile, when he returned he said his goodbyes to the diamond buyer, who was without doubt pleased to be getting out of the place in one piece, then turning to Charlie he said 'I could do with you staying around for a few days, there might be a bit of action, a little problem that needs sorting out.'

'I'm not in a rush to go anywhere, I'll get booked into somewhere local, can you change this money I'll have to buy some new clothes as I've brought fuck all with me.'

Jack gave Charlie some money to be going on with until he could change the rest; Charlie went off to book a room then to purchase some new clothes, before finding a bar to lean against for the rest of the night. Jack rang many numbers before eventually tracking down the extremely elusive and the very deadly Max.

'You're a hard man to find Max.'

'I fuckin hope so Jack.' He laughed.

'Without saying to much over the phone, when you met the French feller in Spain, did you see a woman with him by any chance.'

'Yeah, yeah, I know the one you mean, the last time I saw those two they were going swimming.'

There was a pause for a few seconds, Jack knew exactly what Max had meant, and now the riddle of all these attacks upon him were finally making sense. 'You still there Jack?' Max asked.

'Yeah, I'm still here, I was just thinking.'

'What about?'

'Oh, it's nothing to worry about; I'll get back to you if anything develops.' 'No problem Jack, take care.'

'I will.'

The two phones were silenced and Jack went off to see Angel who had left a message saying that he wanted to see him A.S.A.P, when Jack arrived Angel said 'Where the fuck have you been? I've been trying to get hold of you for weeks, what's happening about the cigs, everyone's on my case.'

'Fuckinell, slow down take a breath, I've been out

of the country for a while, I've only just got a message to come and see you.'
'Right okay, I'm stressed.'
'Aren't we all?'
'Not as much as me.'
'You don't know the half.'
'Maybe not, but I've got enough stress of my own to give me a heart attack.'
'Listen mate you've got enough fuckin weight of your own to give you an heart attack.' He laughed causing Angel to grin a little.
'You're a twat Dunkerley.' Angel laughed.
'Ain't that the truth.' He grinned.
'So when's it gonna happen Jack?'
'I've not spoken to a soul about it yet I'll have to get back to you.'
Jack left Angels house and called at a public telephone box to make some calls, to see if he could organise a shipment of cigarettes to the U.K., all the people that he rang said that they'd get back to him. Jack went back to his car and headed for home. Later that day Charlie rang Jack to see what was occurring and after a quick chat they arranged to meet the following day. Charlie got in touch with Pete and organised a lift off him to Jack's house for the following day. When Pete and Charlie arrived at Jack's house, Jack got into Pete's car and told him to head for the Cheshire Cheese pub, 'We can talk in the pub garden while it's not raining for a change.' Jack jested. 'It'll probably piss down as

soon as we get there.' Pete added. A few minutes later as they rounded the bend the full view of the odd-lot sat in a traffic car came into sight, and right on the edge of the tiny car park. 'Keep going Pete, Jack demanded, turn right onto the carriageway, turn again near Just Fiesta's and then swerve into Raddon Court.' Jack ordered. 'On my way Jack.' Pete grinned as they passed the odd-lots fluorescent vehicle. A few minutes later they pulled onto the car park. 'What now?' Pete asked. 'Now, said Jack, we're going in.'
'It's a fuckin furniture shop Jack.' Pete moaned.
'You mean they don't sell beer Pete.' Jack snapped.
Pete looking sheepish turned away so as not to catch Jack's glare.
Jack got out of the car and the other two men followed him into the huge discount warehouse, they walked by garden furniture, cookers, keep fit equipment, fitted kitchens, bathroom suites, and multitudes of appliances, tools and toys. 'Fuckinell Jack its like Aladdin's cave in here.' Laughed Charlie in bemusement. 'There's even more through the back but we're not going that far.' 'Why not?' asked Pete?
'Coz we're going up that steel staircase to the cafe, that's why.' Jack pointed.
'I could have killed a pint.' Pete moaned.
'A good cup of tea will put you right.' Jack

grinned.
Pete's face was a picture, so much so that Charlie who had been looking on in some amusement had to turn away his chuckling face to save any minor embarrassment. The cafe was empty and the men sat in a corner as far away as they could from the women who were serving at the counter so they couldn't be overheard. They spoke in such low voices that they could barely hear each other. Jack explained to the other two that he would also be bringing other people in to help with this plan and the gist of it was that the Gardner brothers were behind the attacks on Jack and that Jack wasn't having any of it, this was going to be a war and a war with a difference, because the Gardeners didn't know that Jack was coming, and if anything he was coming soon. Jack had been in touch with Les Miller a wheeler dealer who worked the same patch as the Gardeners, Les had had many run ins with the Gardeners over territorial patches and it would be no loss to Les if they weren't to be seen again. Les was after all a happy go lucky type of chap who was about to get happier and of course wealthier as the demise of the Gardener brothers would only be a boost to his present business. Les had let Jack know the whereabouts of the Gardeners and more importantly where they would be the following weekend, Jack had only three days to put his plan into action and this was going to be

his course of action. The three men leaned forward and put their heads together, Charlie and Pete listened intently as Jack told them his plan it's like this boys he said...

Saturday night was soon upon them, and Jack put a team of men around the car park to watch out for two particular vehicles, Jack only knew the day and place of this deal but he was unaware of the exact time of the meeting, Jack and his men could only wait and watch. As darkness fell Jack and his men who were sat in the wooded area surrounding the car park, were getting cold and wet, and by nine o'clock most of them were starving hungry too. By this time Jack wondered if the deal was going to go down at all, as his thoughts turned to throwing his hand in for the night, his decision driven by the freezing cold wind that was cutting through the clothes he had on like a hot knife through butter, and the intermittent rain showers helping the wind chill to freeze his damp body, at the very moment that he'd made up his mind to leave, headlights lit up the car park. The Jaguar circled the car park slowly before finally coming to rest in the far corner. It was ten minutes more before the Gardners arrived in their big four-wheel drive; they flashed their lights at the Jaguar before pulling in along side it, there was no movement from either vehicle for a few minutes, then the Jaguar door opened and a man got out, this was followed straight away with someone emerging from the jeep. By now all Jack's men were sat close by and hardly breathing for fear of giving the game away. Two other men emerged, one from either vehicle, the four of them stood at the back of the Jaguar chatting, then one of the men opened the Jaguar boot and all four of them looked into it, the man then shut it again and the four men then went to the rear of the jeep one of the Gardeners opened the jeep's rear door and once again the four men looked in, a few seconds later the door was closed and the four men stood around chatting incessantly. It was obvious to all of the watchers from the darkness that a deal had been done when the four men started shaking hands and patting each other on the shoulders, it was at this moment that two shots rang out cutting through the darkness and felling two of the four men that were on the car park, the other two men tried to take cover, but were soon overpowered by Jack's team of men. They were taken by surprise big time, two of them were injured and two were restrained, a quick phone call from Jack and two minutes later a van pulled onto the car park. B.T. stepped out of the van and declared 'Everything okay?' Jack nodded. The four men were bound and gagged then bundled into the back of the van onto a tarpaulin sheet that had already been laid out in readiness. Jack climbed into the back of the van where the tied up men were making some strange noises, pulling a silenced weapon from his clothing he calmly said, 'This is for Outlaw.' The four glary-eyed men squealed garbled noises and wriggled frantically but to no avail, for soon they were all silenced. BT pulled the corners of the tarpaulin until he'd made what looked like a large envelope that now hid the four bodies from view, with a little help from the others, he ripped up some of the local shrubbery and threw it into the back of the van, BT made arrangements to meet with Jack the following day, at that the van drove away across the car park. The other men emptied the goodies from the Jaguar and put it out of view in the wooded area, Jack took the bag of money from the four-wheel drive and walked back towards the other men, 'Aren't we getting a share of that Jack?' one of the men said.

'No, you're fucking not, this is Outlaws he's earned it and his Mrs is getting it, anyone got any problems with that?'

No one spoke. 'Right, said Jack you two take them vehicles, you know what to do with them. The two men nodded and without saying a word boarded the vehicles and left the car park. Jack made another phone call and a few minutes later another vehicle came onto the car park, the men that were still left loaded the goodies that had been taken from the Jag into the vehicle and it drove away. Jack explained

to the other men that they would be paid as soon as the goodies had been sold; no one had any problems with that. Jack and Pete talked to each other as they followed the other men the half a mile back to where their vehicles had been left earlier, far enough away not to be noticed yet close enough, if it had come to needing a speedy getaway. The next day Pete went to sell the goodies and to pay off the men while Jack went to see Angel to give him the good news that there were two truckloads of cigs coming and they were both coming to him, Jack explained that he was going away for a few days maybe a week or two and that he would do whatever was necessary for him to do by phone. Angel was at last a happy man, and Jack knew that he could rely on him; so to leave him in charge while he was away was not going to become stressful. Jack met up with Pete later in the day and said, 'Go and pack your bags Pete we'll go away for a few days.'
'What just the two of us?'
'No, bring your Mrs, I'll bring mine, I'll have to sweet talk her mum into having the kids for a few days, but I don't see a problem.'
 'Yeah, right, I'll have some of that.' Pete said daydreaming of sunnier climates.
'Okay, be at mine tomorrow at twelve o'clock in a taxi and don't forget to bring your passport.'
'I won't.' he shouted as he headed for his car.

By three thirty the following afternoon, the two wives who had by now consumed a bit of holiday alcohol were whispering and giggling like schoolgirls, it would be another hour before the plane landed at Malaga airport. As they were going up in the lift to the two apartments that Jack had rented, he said that he had a treat for them the following day as he had borrowed a large motor yacht from a friend for a couple of days. The following morning they had breakfast together and then while Sandra and Jane sat around the pool Jack and Pete said that they would make sure that the boat was okay and that they would meet the girls at the marina at two o'clock, The two men checked the boat over, there wasn't a thing out of place, while Jack lay on the deck soaking up the sun, Pete had another look around, he came across a cupboard in the main bedroom that would not open. He went to the kitchen and took a knife from the drawer, he went back to the bedroom and fiddled with the locked cupboard until it opened, and when it did, just as he'd expected it contained the yacht's armoury of several weapons from a couple of handguns to a few rifles plus a large stock of ammunition, Pete locked the door and went back on deck. Pete told Jack that he was going to get some cigarettes and that he would be back in a while, Jack just waved from his comfortable position in the sun. Pete dashed back to the hotel and on

finding that the wives had gone back to their rooms to have a break from the sun before going out on the yacht in the afternoon, Pete hatched a little plan. It was nearly one o'clock when Pete and Jane arrived at the yacht, and Pete had to shake Jack several times to wake him. 'What's going on?' Jack shouted as he jumped up. 'You're gonna burn Jack, falling asleep in the sun like that.'
'I wasn't asleep was I?'
Pete and Jane laughed and Jack realising that he had been asleep sheepishly grinned.
'Where's Sandra?' Jack asked.
'She's not coming, Pete answered, she's got an headache.' 'Must be the sun.' Jack mumbled.
'Aye it must be.' Pete nodded.
'We might as well get away then, no point in hanging about.'
Within minutes they set sail from the Marina.
'Where to Pete?' Jack asked.
'Head for morocco Jack, it'll be a laugh.'
While the two men had been talking Jane had busied herself around the yacht, she'd give it a good inspection and now she returned with three cups of coffee.
'Couldn't you find any beer?' Pete moaned.
Coffee's fine for me. Jack laughed.
An hour and a half later and they were right out at sea Jack turned the motors off just to sit around for a while and enjoy the tranquility.
'Should I drop anchor Jack?' Pete shouted.

'No point here Pete the water's much to deep.' 'Oh right.' Pete said thoughtfully. Back on the marina Sandra was walking up and down trying to find the yacht that she was supposed to going out on with Jack, Pete and Jane, she was not happy at being unable to find any of the three or the yacht.

Pete went below deck and when he returned he was carrying a pistol, Jack was lay on his sun bed with his eyes shut so he didn't notice the gun, Jane was standing at the side of the yacht admiring the peacefulness she turned around and saw Pete with the gun and shrieked 'What are you doing with that?' At the sound of Jane's shriek Jack sat bolt upright and opened his eyes. 'What the fucks going on Pete?'

'We've got a little problem Jack.' Pete said as he waved the gun about. 'A problem Pete, what problem, everything's sweet we've got our few bob off the diamonds and our other deals, a few bob off the Gardeners, we've got two loads of cigs to pick money up from, we're retired Pete all the works over.'

'Not quite Jack, remember all the times when you only told me where you'd be and time after time there would be some lunatics trying to run you over or shoot you or basically beat you to death, and only I knew where you'd be, it's down to me Jack it's my fault. Pete's face froze he stared at Jack as he raised the pistol, 'This is gonna be hard for me Jack but it's got to be

done.' Then without another word he turned and shot Jane, he ran to her and put another shot in her head.
'Are you fuckin mad.' Jack screamed.
'She's the one Jack, she was fuckin the doorman behind my back, I've known for about a week, but I wasn't sure what I was going to do until today.'
'Fuckinell Pete I'm sorry.'
'So am I Jack he was the bastard who was feeding the information on you to the Gardeners, so every time I said to her that I was just nipping here there and everywhere to meet with you, she was feeding the information to that bastard. 'It's a fuckin hard life Pete.'
'It's gonna get easier Jack.'
'Fuckin right, let's get rid of this fuckin body.'
Pete looked at Jack and forced a smile.

Shadow Man: Jack

Sandra:

Shadow Man: Big Dave

Shadow Man: The Legendary Stevie 'O'

Stevie and Janette Okuefuna's wedding

A young Charles dancing with his niece Louise.

Shadow Man: The mighty Billy Outlaw

Shadow Man: Billy Outlaw

Billy Outlaws funeral

Billy Outlaws final resting place Exeter Devon.

Printed in Great Britain
by Amazon.co.uk, Ltd.,
Marston Gate.